The characters and events in this ...
similarities to real persons, living or dead, is coincidental and not intended by the author.

First published in 2022 by DarkLit Press
Edited by Georgia Papoulias

PRAISE FOR
THIS IS WHERE WE TALK THINGS OUT

"In her debut novella, *This is Where We Talk Things Out*, Caitlin Marceau has crafted one of the most horrifying reads of the year. A fast paced plot and increasing tension from the first chapter made the pages fly by, while her gift for making readers care about her characters in such a brief story raised the stakes all the more. With relatable scenarios that dug ever deeper into danger, I raced to the end, too tense to keep going, but impossible to put down."

—Laurel Hightower, author of *Crossroads* and *Below*.

"Emotionally claustrophobic and unnerving. Takes dysfunctional family to a whole new level."

—Ali Seay, author of *To Offer Her Pleasure*.

"*This is Where We Talk Things Out* by Caitlin Marceau is a winter storm knocking on your door, and the chills it has brought are not ones you can escape. If *Misery,* "A Rose for Emily", and *Mommie Dearest* had a lovechild, here it is. A genuinely upsetting horror novella that holds nothing back. This page-turner will have you devouring the book in a day or two, but you won't be able to stop thinking about it for weeks. Marceau is a dynamite force to keep an eye on."

— Sara Tantlinger, Bram Stoker Award-winning author of *The Devil's Dreamland.*

"Marceau is one of the most chilling new voices in horror."

— Lindy Ryan, author of *Bless Your Heart.*

BOOKS BY
CAITLIN MARCEAU

Palimpsest
23 McCormick Road
Magnum Opus
A Blackness Absolute

This is Where We Talk Things Out

Caitlin Marceau

DarkLit Press

CONTENT WARNING

The story that follows may contain graphic violence and gore.

Please go to the very back of the book for more detailed content warnings.

Beware of spoilers.

To my mom and dad,
Thanks for not being
f*cking crazy.

To Kyle,
Thanks for being there
when our parents were
absolutely f*cking crazy.

CONTENTS

THURSDAY, JANUARY 13, 7:18 P.M.

"Why are you giving that bitch your time?"

"That *bitch* is my mother, so watch your mouth."

"Sorry, why are you giving that bitch, *your mother*, your time? Better?"

Miller turns to look at Florence, crossing her arms in front of her chest and waiting for the other woman to apologize. When her fiancée makes no move to retract the comment, she rolls her eyes and goes back to looking through her side of the bedroom closet. She can feel Florence staring at her, the strength of her gaze practically boring holes through her sensitive skin, and the hair on the back of Miller's neck bristles in response.

"I just can't understand how you're letting her weasel her way back into your life," Florence finally says to the back of Miller's head. "After all the shit she put you through, put *us* through—"

"I'm not letting her back, I'm—"

"—and after all the work you've done—"

"—just trying to find some middle ground—"

"—to put up those boundaries—"

"—with her."

"—I can't believe you're just letting her win."

Miller shakes her head in frustration. She grabs one of the thick sweaters from the back of the closet, tries not to stretch the neck wider as she pulls it off its metal hanger, and begins to fold it as she turns back to face her partner.

"She's not winning, Flor. We're just talking things out."

"It feels like she is. By agreeing to this weekend, you've basically told her that if she doesn't get her way at first, then she can harass you as much as she wants until she finally does."

Miller rolls her eyes in protest, but knows there's a hint of truth to what Florence tells her.

It had started innocently enough: a call from a number she didn't recognize. Not wanting to deal with spam calls or telemarketers, she had let it go to voicemail. When she'd eventually played the message back, it was from Sylvie, her mother, who she'd cut off all contact from a few years earlier. She'd been tempted to block the number, but thoughts of what had happened last March—only a few months shy of a year ago—had stopped her cold and, instead, she'd deleted the voicemail.

Then Sylvie had started texting her. At first, it was just once to let her know that she'd changed phone numbers. Then it was once a day to tell her she missed her. Then it was practically every hour to tell her how much she loved her "little girl," words that would have meant something to her long ago, but were now too little too late. When the texting and constant phone calls had become overwhelming, Miller had finally blocked the number and hoped to put the situation behind her. She'd felt silly for not having done it sooner, and had hoped that Florence wouldn't find out about her moment of weakness when it came to keeping Sylvie at bay.

Unfortunately, things had gone from bad to worse when Sylvie eventually found her on social media. Miller had been flooded with notifications as her mother left her comments, sent her private messages, and even tagged her in old photos. Even when she blocked her mother, a new account would get created and the harassment would resume within a day. Miller had figured out that the quickest way to avoid Sylvie on social media was to stop using it, so she'd deleted her accounts and made new ones with fake names.

That didn't dissuade Sylvie, though.

Miller's mother had taken the liberty of reaching out to a few of her acquaintances, who were more than happy to give Sylvie her daughter's work address so she could surprise her with a visit when she came to town. She'd even called Miller's boss, who gave her an extended lunch so she could spend time with her beloved mom, unaware that Miller had done everything in her power to avoid seeing her face-to-face.

It was only when Sylvie followed Miller home after work one evening that the two of them had finally talked things out in the parking lot.

"She's just trying to mend fences now that my dad's gone," Miller says.

"Is she? Or is she trying to guilt you into taking her bullshit now that he's not around to listen to it?"

Miller throws her arms in the air, the sweater that she'd meticulously folded coming undone, and looks at Florence.

"So what do you want me to do?"

"To *not* go! Tell her to fuck off and that you're staying home."

"So that she can keep calling me? So that she can keep showing up unannounced at my work? So that she can figure out which unit we live in and show up at our door? Or, God help us, show up at our wedding without an invitation? Is that what you want?"

"Who says she's not going to do all of this *anyway*?"

Miller sighs and takes a seat at the end of the mattress, her toes skimming the floor as she sits on the massive California king-size bed that fills their too-small bedroom to bursting.

"You're right, but I don't know what else to do."

"Just don't go."

"But I *want* to go, Flor," Miller confesses. "We're getting married in, like, two months, and I don't have anyone coming."

"That's not true, babe. We have our friends coming and—"

"*We* have *our* friends coming. And you have pretty much your entire family showing up too. And I have… who, exactly? I don't have any grandparents left, Sylvie's an only child, my dad's family lives in France and didn't give a fuck about us even when he was alive, and it's not like I'm rolling in siblings. I don't have anyone, Flor."

"You have me."

"That's great. Are you going to fill my half of the venue in addition to marrying me? Should we call the caterer and ask them to double the entrees?"

"You know what I mean."

"And you know what *I* mean. Sylvie's the only relative I have left and it seems like she really wants to fix things. And I want to fix them too. I've already told her that if we can't come to some kind of an understanding, that if she can't respect the choices I've made and the life I have, then we're done. She's out. That's it, that's all."

"Do you think she'd really be able to respect that decision?"

"Fuck no. But if she can't, then I can always get a restraining order or something. I don't know, we'll figure it out if the time comes."

Florence inhales through her nose and lets out a heavy sigh through her mouth before taking a seat on the bed next to Miller. She wraps her arms around her fiancée's narrow shoulders and kisses her temple gently.

"Okay."

"That's it?" Miller asks, surprised.

"Look, I can't pretend to understand why you want to salvage whatever it is you have with Sylvie. But I love you and I respect you enough to trust you on this. If you think this is what's best, if this is something you *really* want, then I think you should go for it. I also think you need to prepare for what happens if she disappoints you again. This isn't the first time she's tried to work things out with you, but I think, for your sake, that it needs to be the last."

Miller nods her head before leaning it against Florence's shoulder. The two of them sit together on the bed in comfortable silence before Florence grabs the sweater from Miller's lap and starts folding it.

"So where exactly is she taking you?"

"I have no idea," Miller admits, pushing herself up from the edge of the mattress and making her way back to the closet. "Somewhere up north."

"That's specific."

Miller laughs as she pulls another sweater off its hanger. "All I know is that she's taking me up north this weekend for some mother-daughter bonding time."

Florence leans over and slides her phone out from her pocket before sitting up again. She unlocks the device and opens the weather app with a frown.

"And you're sure she said this weekend, right?"

"Yeah. Why?"

"It's supposed to storm," she says, swiping through the map to see the expected snowfall across the province.

"It's Québec, what else is new?"

"It's supposed to be really bad, babe. Like, they're anticipating a full white-out. Maybe ask her to push it to next weekend?"

Miller laughs. It's a single "ha" that seems to catch her by surprise. "If I do that, she'll think I'm trying to weasel out of seeing her. It's just not worth the headache."

Miller grabs a few more sweaters, some fleece-lined jeans, warm leggings, and some loungewear, piling it onto the bed. Florence, not wanting to be unhelpful, gets the small black duffel bag out from the closet in the entranceway of their condo and helps her partner pack her clothing away in the worn bag. Together, they pack up Miller's extra toiletries and her outerwear and set aside her extra warm boots before curling up on the couch with a movie.

As the two slowly drift asleep in the soft glow of the television and the warmth of their sherpa blanket, snow begins to fall outside.

FRIDAY, JANUARY 14, 2:45 P.M.

Miller doesn't need to see the red Toyota Yaris pull into the parking lot to know it's fifteen minutes early. Sylvie has never been known to be late and, as Miller expects, the familiar double-honk of the car rings out letting her know Sylvie's waiting.

"You have everything?" Florence asks as Miller pulls on her boots from the entranceway.

"I hope so!"

"Did you pack enough socks?"

"Yup!"

"You've got your ski pants?"

"Yeah."

"Did you pack your phone charger?"

"Uh, I'm not sure actually."

"It's a trick question," Florence says with a smile. "I slipped it in your bag this morning when I saw you forgot it."

"Well that's because you're perfect."

"Duh. I just don't like to brag; it ruins my humble appearance."

The two of them laugh and, not for the first time, Miller wishes she didn't have to leave.

As if she can read her mind, Florence wraps her arms around Miller's neck once she's done pulling on her boots, and she kisses her gently. "Are you sure you want to do this?"

"No, but I'm going to do it anyway. It's the right thing to do."

"And you're sure I can't convince you to stay home with me?"

"I mean, you could convince me to do just about anything if you really tried—"

"Is that right?"

"—so I *hope* you don't try too hard."

Florence sighs, defeated. "Alright, alright. Have fun with Sylvie."

"I'll try!"

"Fingers crossed."

Miller wraps her arms around Florence and kisses her back, hard, before picking up her black duffel bag.

"Text me when you get up there, okay?" Florence asks.

"I will."

"And you'll send me the address when she gives it to you?"

"Of course."

"If anything, *anything* goes wrong or you want to come home or—"

"I'll call you.

"Promise?"

"Promise."

Miller opens the door and steps out into the hall of the complex. She leans into the condo to reach for the doorknob and Florence gives one last forlorn sigh before pretending to swoon against a wall, her hand draped across her forehead as she dramatically turns her face away from Miller and begins singing Eric Carmen's "All By Myself."

"Love you!" Miller laughs, pulling the front door closed behind her.

"Love you too!" Florence shouts back, her reply muffled by the wood.

Miller walks to the elevator, the duffel heavy on her shoulder as she leans forward and presses the round silver button calling the car to her floor. Although her condo has a front door that leads to the parking lot, she doesn't want to help

Sylvie figure out which unit she calls home. At least not until she sees how the weekend alone with her goes.

The doors to the elevator slide open, Miller steps inside, and they shut behind her as she presses the button marked 'RC,' *rez-de-chaussée*, to take her to the ground floor. She rolls her shoulder, trying to find a comfortable spot for the heavy bag to rest, eyeing the tiled floor. Although the trip down is short, she debates putting her bag down to give her shoulder a break, but the doors open and let her out into the lobby before she gets a chance to make up her mind.

Her winter boots drag as she trudges across the open space, her rubber heels scraping against the rough pile of the black carpets that protect the expensive tiling of the building's foyer and trap the melted snow and salt brought in off the road from mid November until early May. The ground level of the building always becomes a checkerboard of black carpeting and eggshell flooring for six months out of the year, clashing with the complex's luxurious interior and sleek advertisements designed to sell the place as an upscale condominium.

As she passes her mailbox on the way out, she debates pulling off the nameplate which proudly reads "Unit 32: Florence Laroux and Miller Cranshaw" to prevent Sylvie from finding her when things go sideways.

If *they go sideways*, she reminds herself.

Although she hopes that the weekend with her mother will go well, there's a knot in the pit of her stomach, and she can't help but feel like she's making a mistake by giving into Sylvie. It's not the first time she's been guilted into seeing the woman, despite her better judgement. Growing up, her mom had always made a point of overstepping Miller's boundaries and expecting her actions to result in few consequences. She'd always apologize and beg for her daughter to give her a chance to make things right, for them to "start fresh." And while Sylvie had a bad habit of extending poison ivy disguised as olive branches, Miller had a worse habit of accepting them.

She pushes open the first set of glass doors, the entrance significantly colder than the lobby, before opening the second set and heading out into the parking lot. It's cold out, and even though it's exactly as frigid as she'd planned for, the brisk air still manages to surprise her.

Her mom honks twice at her—Miller's not sure if Sylvie's worried she won't be able to find the familiar red car in the half-empty parking lot or if she's urging her daughter to walk faster—and waves at her through the glass. As Miller approaches the Yaris, Sylvie pushes on a button by the window and the vehicle clicks as the doors unlock. She opens her window a crack, clearly not wanting to expose herself to the below-zero air more than she has to.

"Just put your stuff in the back seat. I already have things in the trunk."

"Okay."

The window hums as it closes.

Miller opens the back door on her mother's side.

"Oh, put it on your side," Sylvie tells Miller, turning to look at her over her shoulder. "I like having my purse behind me in case I need it."

"Okay."

Miller closes the door and walks around to the passenger's side, opens the back door, and puts her duffel bag on the seat.

"Can you put it on the floor? I don't want you getting dirt on the seat."

"Why would I get dirt on the seat?"

"In case you dragged your bag on the ground or something. I don't want you getting road salt on the upholstery."

"Why would I drag my bag on the ground?" Miller asks, confused by Sylvie's train of thought.

"I don't know! But hurry up, you're freezing out the car!"

Miller wants to argue, but she isn't sure if it's because Sylvie's request is unreasonable (it isn't) or if it's because she's used to pushing back against whatever her mother says (she is), so she bites her tongue and puts the duffel bag on the floor of the car before getting into the passenger's seat.

"Hi!" Sylvie cries, as if the last minute of conversation never happened. She unbuckles her seatbelt and leans across the small space to give Miller an awkward one-armed hug. While it's far less enthusiastic on her side, Miller returns the gesture.

"Hey."

"I'm so glad you agreed to come out for the weekend. *So* glad! It's going to be great!"

"Yeah, it'll be nice to get away from the city," Miller says unconvincingly. "Where exactly is the cabin, by the way? Florence wants to know."

"Why?" Sylvie's tone is immediately different at the mention of Florence's name. "So she can show up uninvited in the middle of our time together?"

"No. So she knows where I'm going to be all weekend."

"It's up north."

"I know it's up north, but *where* up north?"

Sylvie shrugs. "I don't know the exact township because it's between two of them."

"Okay," Miller says slowly, "but which two?"

"I can't remember the names, but they're French. Saint-Something-de-Something or whatever. I'll have to check the map."

"Okay… so check the map."

"I'll do it when we get there," Sylvie says dismissively.

"Can you just do it now?"

"We're already running late, Miller, because *someone* doesn't know how to be on time," she snaps, grabbing the gearshift and taking the car out of 'park' and putting it into 'drive.' "I was waiting for like twenty minutes."

Miller frowns, pointing at the clock on the dashboard, the green light glowing softly against the black screen. "It's not even three."

“And I’ve been here since almost two-thirty,” Sylvie lies.

Miller exhales slowly and plasters a smile on. “Okay, we’ll check the map later.”

Sylvie nods enthusiastically and steps on the gas, moving the car out of its parking spot and towards the road. As much as Miller knows her mom is wrong, she knows whatever she says now will set the tone for the entire weekend. If she wants to make things work with Sylvie, and she *really* does, she knows she’ll need to swallow her pride and do everything she can to meet the woman halfway.

She just hopes she’s not the only one trying.

Sylvie pulls the Yaris out of the lot and towards the highway, and Miller watches as the condo fades from view in the rearview mirror.

AIRBAG

FRIDAY, JANUARY 14, 4:27 P.M.

The snow falls heavier than when Miller and Sylvie first hit the road. It comes down in sheets, which drape the trees and mountainside in a blanket of white. Even the pines lose some of their resilient green as the snow coats the branches and bleaches away their colour. The clouds hang low in the burnt umber sky, the sun almost done tucking itself out of view despite how early in the evening it still is. Miller watches as flakes of snow hit the window, perfect geometric wonders, before melting against glass warmed by the car's heater.

As much as Miller likes being out of the city, driving on country roads and lonely strips of highway make her nervous this far north. The lights that normally bathe the road in a soft amber glow don't extend this far out into the middle of nowhere, and the strips of pavement are unkempt and desperate for repair. The car bounces and shakes over the uneven ground, tires hitting potholes and deep cracks, as Sylvie speeds onwards.

"Are we almost there yet?" Miller asks.

Her mother laughs.

"It's been a long time since I've heard you ask me that question."

Miller smiles. "I guess it has."

The two of them drive in silence for a bit.

"Remember that trip we took to Edmonton?" Sylvie asks.

"Which one? Dad took us on so many."

"The one where he insisted we *drive* the whole way down."

Miller cracks up, the memory catching her by surprise. "Oh my God, yes! He wanted us to take the shitty Windstar there and back because it was 'dependable' and could fit all our bags and souvenirs."

"With leg room," Sylvie quips.

"Yes! He was obsessed with the leg room the entire way down. Wasn't it, like, the entire reason he didn't want to take a plane?"

Sylvie shakes her head. "He made it seem that way, but I think he just didn't want to spend the money on a flight."

"Joke was on him," Miller cackles, remembering how the van broke down only a day out of Montreal. It's never stopped being funny that not only had he had to pay for the dead vehicle to be towed to a garage, but he also ended up having to buy their flights to and from Edmonton (*"They call* this *leg room?"*), pay baggage fees from overstuffed suitcases (in both directions), and buy a whole new car when he finally returned home.

"He was so mad," Sylvie agrees. "Here he is, just trying to save a buck, and he ends up spending three times as much. God, he's funny."

"Yeah, he really was."

Was.

It's heavy in the air and hangs painfully between them. Sylvie turns her attention back to the road ahead of her, while Miller goes back to looking out the window on the passenger's side as a lump forms in the back of her throat and her mouth suddenly feels too dry. She wants to say something, anything, to cut the tension, but she just watches the hills and trees blur together in the snow as the car speeds onwards.

"We aren't," Sylvie says suddenly.

"What?"

"You asked if we were almost there. We aren't."

"Oh, that's too bad. It'll be nice to get unpacked and warmed up."

"Are you cold?"

"No, no, I'm fine."

"You just said you wanted to get warmed up."

"Yeah, but like, I just mean I'm excited to get into a warm cabin to get all cosy."

"Okay, but if you're cold, I can put the heat up."

"No, I'm fine," Miller reiterates. "I'm just eager to get in."

"Here, let me—" Sylvie says, reaching a hand out to crank the heat up even higher.

Miller puts her hand over the dial to stop her. "Sylvie, don't. I said I'm fine."

The older woman swallows loudly, the corners of her mouth drawing down into a scowl. "Don't call me that."

"Call you what?"

"Sylvie."

"That's your name."

"Not to you. I'm 'Mom' to you."

Miller rolls her eyes and goes back to looking out the window.

"I *am* 'Mom' to you still," Sylvie pushes, "even if you don't like it. It's just a fact."

"You're my mother, Sylvie, but you haven't been my mom for years."

"Really? That's how you want to start our weekend off? By telling me I'm not your mother?"

Miller sighs.

"Look, can we just talk about this another time?" she asks.

"Talk about what? The fact that I'm not your 'mom' or the fact that, for some reason, you seem to hate me so much that you want to cut me out of your life forever?"

"I don't hate you," Miller says with an eye roll.

"It feels like you do."

"Okay, but how you feel doesn't dictate the truth of the situation."

Sylvie laughs in disbelief. "Okay, so not only are you attacking me, you're trying to tell me that I'm crazy for how I feel."

"What are you talking about? That's not what I said!"

"Oh, sorry, I guess I'm an idiot too, right?"

"I just meant that—"

"Not all of us could afford a university education, Miller. We didn't all have parents that paid our way through school. Some of us had to actually work for what we have," Sylvie practically spits at her. "I'm sorry that means I'm not as smart as you."

Miller's mouth tightens as her mother shouts, all the unspoken anger she's ever felt threatening to choke her. Her heart beats faster as she remembers the long days at school and longer nights working, not just so she could pay tuition but so she could help pay the mortgage. Even with healthcare, her father's early-onset Alzheimer's had forced him from work and drained the family financially. Every hour Miller hadn't spent studying, she'd spent working to pay the long-overdue bills. Even though he'd been sick for almost a decade, Sylvie had refused to work or spend time away from him, claiming she didn't want him to forget her (he did) or for his final moments to be spent alone. Miller grips the leather armrest tight, her short nails threatening to pierce the fabric as she tries to calm down.

I wish it had been—

She stops herself.

The words taste like bile and the pressure to let them out is astounding, but Miller swallows them instead, their acrid flavour leaving a bad taste in her mouth.

She finally settles on a dispassionate "whatever" before turning her attention back to the window.

"Do you even want to be here?" Sylvie asks, trying to keep the fight between them alive.

"What?"

"It just feels like you don't want to be here and—you know what? Never mind. Just, never mind." Sylvie shakes her head to herself.

"What is it?" Miller pushes.

She expects Sylvie to resist her prodding a little longer; she's used to the older woman goading her into conversation when she's feeling especially dramatic. Instead, the older woman shakes her head back and forth, the straw-blonde, grey-threaded hair swinging stiffly. Miller's amazed there's any movement left in the woman's hair at all, given how much spray Sylvie's always used on the pin-straight locks that hang halfway down her back. Growing up, Sylvie had always talked about how she never needed to dye or style her mane and that people loved her hair because it was "straight as an arrow, thick as a hedge, and gold like spun sunshine." Miller would always nod agreeingly, having never seen it as any of those things for as long as she'd been alive. It had only ever looked grey and lifeless to her.

"It just doesn't feel like you're even trying, is all."

Is all. She says it so casually, but Miller knows it's anything but. It's Sylvie laying the groundwork in case things don't work out and she needs to point fingers. It's Sylvie preparing for the worst, but trying to position herself in a way that lets her shift the blame for a failed weekend onto Miller.

"You're right."

"So you agree that you're not trying?" Sylvie asks, voice laced with excitement.

"You're right that I don't want to be here."

Miller doesn't want to get into another fight, not when she's already so tired of the weekend before it's even really started, so she pulls out a set of headphones from her jacket pocket and stuffs the buds into her ears. She connects the cable to her phone and plays music as she looks back out at the countryside, the haunting voice of Hozier soothing her.

Sylvie drives in silence.

Friday, January 14, 9:32 P.M.

The car jolts to a stop and wakes Miller up from her nap, her face pressed against the cold glass of the passenger's side window. She must have drifted off as Sylvie drove, the swaying of the car and the gentle music from her headphones lulling her to sleep. The sky is black, or at least she thinks it is; it's hard to tell with all the snow falling, the heavy wind, and the branches from all the trees obscuring her view.

She turns her music off and puts her headphones back in her pocket as Sylvie reaches across the small space to tap her on the leg.

"We're here, sleepyhead," she says excitedly.

Miller nods with a yawn, still craving sleep. She stretches her arms out in front of her and works the slight kink out of her neck as her mom turns off the engine, pulling the key from the ignition and slipping it into her pants pocket. She opens her door, a blast of ice-cold air pushing its way into the car and blowing into Miller's open coat, chilling her to the core. She shivers, breath suddenly visible, and pulls the parka closed with one hand as she zips it up to her chin with the other. Despite the falling snow, it had been easy to forget it was winter thanks to the warmth inside the Yaris.

"I'll meet you inside," Sylvie says as she gets out of the car.

"Do you need any help with your bags?" Miller offers, in the interest of making up for their earlier argument.

"I don't have any, but I appreciate it!" Sylvie says with a smile. "I'm going to go make sure the heat's on in all the rooms, so I'll meet you inside."

Miller nods as Sylvie closes the car door behind her. She ties back her thick blonde curls before she pulls her tuque on—otherwise the hat wouldn't fit on her head—and makes sure her gloves are secured before opening the car door, a process made difficult by the strong winds. She grabs her bag from behind the backseat, the door trying to shut on her as she pulls out the duffel by its strap, before turning her attention to the building.

Like most of the cabins in the area, this one is old and weathered, the Western Red Cedar having seen more winters in its lifetime than either Miller or Sylvie have. The building is wide but not very tall, the second floor likely just a pair of small rooms with angled ceilings. Because of the uneven ground, the front half of the cabin rests on wooden supports drilled into the hillside and a solid cement foundation. Although the structure is technically big enough to accommodate a family looking for a woodsy getaway, Miller suspects the space will begin to feel small after a few short days with her mother.

She breathes a sigh, glad that she won't be spending more than the weekend here.

The path that leads to the cabin is narrow and icy, the snow only making the frozen ground more treacherous, and the stairs leading up to the front door aren't much better. Miller clings to the railing with her free hand and hopes that Sylvie remembered to bring salt as she carefully ascends. As she approaches, the front light of the cabin turns on and the soft yellow light temporarily blinds her. She stops in her tracks, blinking as her eyes adjust, before slowly continuing up the stairs. She pauses in front of the door to catch her breath before pushing her way inside.

Miller's not sure what she was expecting the interior to look like, but it definitely wasn't this. In fact, it might have been anything *but* this.

home

The entranceway is painted a soft eggshell, a row of brass coat hooks lining the wall beside her. She looks down at the blue doormat she's standing on, lifting one foot at a time to make sure her eyes aren't playing tricks on her as she admires the bluejays and branches that decorate the small carpet. It's the same one she used to wipe her shoes on when she was a kid, the same one that rested on the floor of her childhood home's eggshell-white entranceway. Even the brass hooks are familiar, as is the hand-woven straw basket by the door holding gloves, scarves, and hats of all colours.

Miller drops her duffel onto the ground and kicks off her boots, advancing deeper into the cabin with her jacket still on. Although it's not a carbon copy of her old house—the layout and construction of the cabin is different from that of the suburban bungalow she grew up in—it's as close to it as possible given the circumstances.

She drifts through the living room, her chest tightening as she walks by the pair of leather La-Z-Boys her parents used to sit in while watching late-night TV when she was small, the brown leather couch she used to fall asleep on when she got home from school across the room from them. Everything in the space is familiar to her: the beige carpet she used to do homework on, the oval coffee table with the rose carvings across the top, the crooked photos mounted on the beige walls, the off-white throw pillows littering the sofa, even the worn in ottoman she always hit her pinky on.

She moves into the kitchen already knowing what she'll find: cupboards painted bright white with blue handles, familiar coffee mugs and tea cups hanging in rows on the wall, the pantry doors painted blue to match the cupboard hardware, the worn wooden island in the centre of the room with its shaky wheels and careless knife marks etched across the top, the blue and white striped canisters holding coffee and teas next to the ancient drip-machine and stove-top kettle. Even the plates in the drying rack by the sink are familiar, with their cracks and chips and imperfections.

"What the fuck?"

"Language," Sylvie calls from the kitchen sink as she washes her hands, pumping soap from a white dispenser shaped like a finch. She's wearing a small apron with paw prints embroidered around the hem and has a blue tea towel thrown over her shoulder: a familiar uniform from the days that she used to greet Miller at the end of her journey home from school through the bracing cold or blistering heat.

"What is all this?"

"What do you mean?"

"What do I mean? *What do I mean?*" Miller half shouts, gesturing around the small space with gloved hands. "I *mean* why does this place look like our old house? *How* does it look like our old house? Didn't you and dad get rid of this shit years ago when you moved?"

Sylvie shakes her head. "We couldn't bring most of it to the new place because of how much smaller the apartment was compared to the house, but we put a lot of it in storage."

"Why?"

Sylvie shrugs. "I guess I hoped that when he got better we'd move back into a house one day."

Miller sighs. It was clear from her dad's diagnosis that he was never going to get better. It seemed like everyone but Sylvie had known this.

"Okay, but why is all this stuff *here*? The person you're renting this place from doesn't mind?" she says, confused, still not understanding.

Sylvie shakes her head. "I'm not renting this place, Miller. I bought this place."

"You bought a cabin?"

"Yeah."

"You? *You* bought a cabin?"

"Yes! My therapist thought—"

"*You* go to therapy?"

"—it might be nice for me to have a place that I could go to get away from the stress of everything since I was having a hard time living in the apartment without Robert. So I took a trip up here this past summer and liked it so much that I bought the place."

"And then filled it with stuff from our old house?"

"I thought it might be nice to fill the place up with happy memories. You know, from when we were all a family together. Do you like it?"

"It's definitely something."

Sylvie smiles, drying her hands off on a dish towel hanging from the oven handle. "Go get settled and I'll make us dinner."

"Honestly, I'm exhausted," Miller lies, "so I think I'm just going to go to bed."

"Oh, okay," Sylvie says, plainly disappointed. "Well then how about I make you some hot chocolate? I know how much you enjoy it."

"Oh, that's really sweet, but I'm honestly too tired for even that."

Miller doesn't tell Sylvie that she hasn't enjoyed hot chocolate in years. When she started dating Florence—a diabetic—she'd stopped eating sweet foods and could no longer stand the taste of them. It's something she finds especially funny given her sweet tooth growing up, but she's kept it from Sylvie given how much her mother hates her partner.

She also doesn't tell Sylvie that she's wide awake and freaked out by the unexpected trip down memory lane.

Sylvie's frown deepens. "Okay, well, your bedroom is down the hall past the living room. You'll see a bathroom first and then it's just at the end of the small hallway."

"Great, thanks."

"If you need anything, I'll be upstairs in my bedroom. It's just at the top," she tells her, pointing to the small staircase opposite the living room, "and then the first door on the left."

"Sounds good."

"I love you, sweetie. Sleep well."

"'Night Sylvie," Miller says, turning around and heading back to the entranceway. She unzips her coat and hangs it on one of the brass hooks before pulling off her tuque and gloves, throwing them into the straw basket by the door. She moves her boots from the familiar mat to the black plastic shoe holder and heads to her bedroom for the weekend.

As she moves through the cabin that looks so much like her old house, the hairs on the back of her neck stand at attention. There's something about these old familiar things that just feels wrong. *Unnatural*, she thinks.

It's her house, but it isn't.

It's her childhood, but it's not.

She passes by the bathroom Sylvie mentioned and can't help but pop her head inside to see what it looks like. As expected, it's a carbon copy of the second-floor washroom from her parent's old home. There's a '90s-looking toilet seat cover made of green fabric and a matching mint bath rug on the tiled floor. The hand towels, which hang on a white bar fixed to the wall, sport a white and green gingham pattern that matches the bath towels on the back of the shower door. On the vanity counter in front of the mirror rests a white ceramic bowl shaped like a giant scallop and filled with decorative soaps shaped like shells (exclusively for decoration) beside a bottle of foaming soap (actually allowed to be used). There's also a small basket holding brushes, combs, and hair elastics, along with a half-empty bottle of body lotion. On the small shelf above the toilet are jars of expensive face creams, a bottle of perfume, cosmetics that were discontinued years ago, and some hand cream.

It's a lot to process so, instead, Miller focuses on just getting to her bedroom so she can relax.

Unfortunately, Miller quickly realises that that's unlikely to happen as her eyes fall upon the carnation-pink wallpaper with the white polka dots through the open door. She looks into the room, her head spinning, and wishes very badly that she was back home with Florence.

The room is exactly as she remembers it: the white vanity her dad made her for her sweet-sixteen along with its matching chair, the small dresser with her glass touch-lamp resting on top of it, the twin bed she used to sleep in with its rose patterned comforter and the quilt her grandmother gave her when she was six, and her bookshelf jam packed with books. Sylvie had even put up her old posters, their colours faded and bleached from years of direct sunlight, and Polaroids she'd kept tacked on the wall near her bed.

She sets her duffel bag down on the ground next to the vanity and takes out her cell phone, desperately needing to hear Florence's voice. She dials the number she knows by heart and waits for her fiancée to answer.

"He—o?" Florence says, voice cutting in and out.

"Hey!"

"H—? —ler? Is— you?"

"Hey, babe, can you hear me?"

"What?"

"Can you hear me?"

"I ca—'t h— you. Wha—?

"Ah, damn," Miller says to herself. "I'll let you go babe, the reception is terrible."

"R—ption seem— b—d. I'll let— go. Ok—y? L—ve y—!"

"Love you too, Flo. Sleep well!" Florence hangs up on her before she's finished talking, but Miller continues anyway. "I miss you."

Discouraged but still determined to talk to Florence, Miller writes up a text and hits 'send,' but sighs in frustration when the text won't go through. Outside the cabin, the wind rattles the trees and the glass windowpanes, the snow a heavy spiral of white that covers everything in its path. Miller watches it through the open blinds, awed by its beauty and annoyed by its inconvenience.

Miller puts her phone down on her old nightstand and opens her duffel bag, finding her pyjamas to get ready for bed. As she turns off the lights and slips between the worn bedsheets, she can't help but wonder if she'll even be able to fall asleep in the too familiar bed.

She does.

SATURDAY, JANUARY 15, 2:19 A.M.

It’s not the wind that wakes her up, but the need to pee. Half awake, she stumbles across the bedroom, bumping into furniture that shouldn't be there. When she reaches the hallway, she remembers she’s not home, but is at the cabin. Her heart sinks when she thinks of Florence and their warm bed in the condo, and she makes her way to the washroom at the end of the hall.

She slaps the wall a few times, struggling to find the light, before finally turning it on and making it to the toilet. She washes her hands with the foam soap—not the decorative shell soap—and as she dries her hands on the towels, she realises she’s awake. Painfully, completely, indisputably awake.

She creeps back to her room and sits on the edge of her bed, the ancient mattress creaking under her weight. She takes her phone off the nightstand, the screen lighting up, and checks to see if Florence has answered her text yet.

She hasn’t; the text never sent.

MESSAGE SEND ERROR

Miller rolls her eyes and puts the phone back on the table. The battery is low, but she’s not worried about that thanks to the horrible reception. It’s not like she’d be able to successfully place a call if she wanted to anyway.

Deciding that her room is the last place she wants to be, Miller pulls on a pair of slippers and her warm housecoat, exiting her room to explore the rest of the cabin. As she heads back into the hallway, the floor creaks beneath her. She winces and reminds herself to move slowly. Sylvie's always been a light sleeper.

She passes through the narrow hallway, noticing the linen closet for the first time. She opens the door, already knowing that all too familiar bath towels, facecloths, and bed sheets are inside. The hinge squeaks as the accordion door opens revealing the perfectly folded piles, cotton heaps adorned with faded patterns and accidental bleach spots. She closes the door and moves into the living room, not sure if she wants to curl up on the old sofa or run to the next room.

There's something so unnatural about seeing her childhood repurposed for the cabin's interior. She knows it's Sylvie's way of moving past her grief, but it only serves to wake Miller's own pain back up.

With the snow blocking out the moonlight and hiding the stars, the photos on the wall have hollow eyes and empty smiles. Miller stares at the images of herself when she was just a kid, with her uneven pigtails and collection of too-big t-shirts sporting her favourite Disney princesses. She doesn't remember all of the moments captured on film—she was too young for some of them—but she remembers the photos of those moments from where they lived on the walls of the old house.

But now they're here, in this cabin turned mausoleum.

Her dad is with her in most of them. He holds her in his arms or on his lap, or he balances her small body on top of his shoulders. He was always so happy, so caring, so supportive. He worked as a truck driver and would be gone for days, sometimes weeks, at a time. No matter how long he was gone, when he'd come home he'd scoop her up in a bear hug—lifting her clear off the ground—and tell Miller how much he'd missed her, and how much she'd grown (even if he'd only been gone for the day).

Miller misses her dad. So much so that she wishes—

She shakes her head, trying to stop the thought from forming.

Whenever the thought crosses her mind, she can't help but be disgusted with herself. Looking at the photos of her father in a living room pulled out of her youth, even just the idea of thinking… *it*, makes her feel sick.

She moves to the next cluster of photographs. She's older in these, as is her father, but neither of their smiles quite reach their eyes. His Alzheimer's had progressed alarmingly fast and the older she'd gotten, the faster he had forgotten her. She pauses by the last photo they'd ever taken together, her throat tight as she remembers what he had asked her right before Sylvie snapped the picture.

"Where's Miller?"

I wish it had been—

There it was again. That intrusive thought.

She doesn't want to think about it.

With difficulty, she forces herself away from the photos in the living room and into the kitchen, but even this eerily familiar space is too full of memories for her to stand.

Miller climbs up to the second floor, careful not to tread too heavily on the wooden steps. The last thing she needs is for her mother to chastise her for being awake at two in the morning.

She peeks into the bedroom on the right as she passes the doorway. It's small, with slanted ceilings and a tiny window. The room is packed full of boxes, which Miller can only assume are the remainder of her mother's belongings from the old house: knickknacks that used to have a place in her small home, but were too much for the even smaller cabin. At the back of the room, a small washer and dryer have been hooked up for laundry, the yellowed outer shells giving away the machines' age. Across the hall is her mother's door, which she approaches cautiously.

As she does, the air turns sour. It reminds her of food left in the sun about to spoil. She sniffs the air, the putrid scent getting stronger the closer she gets to her mother's door. She reaches out to grab the handle, wanting to peer inside, but stops suddenly when she hears her mother.

Sylvie's voice is a low mumble, like she's talking in her sleep or whispering with friends. The words sound like they're coming fast, but from Miller's side of the door they're inaudible.

Not wanting to wake the woman up from whatever dream she's having, Miller creeps back down the steps, through the living room, and into her room. Once the door is closed, she tries sending her text to Florence one last time—it's unsuccessful—before going back to an uneasy sleep filled with her father's face and empty smiles.

SATURDAY, JANUARY 15, 9:09 A.M.

The alarm Miller snoozed goes off again. With a groan, she reaches along the nightstand and slaps the screen a handful of times before finally shutting the noise off. She doesn't want to get up early, but she knows how Sylvie is when it comes to "wasting the day." With a deep sigh, she forces herself to sit up and blinks against the harsh sunlight streaming into her room through the thin curtains.

Somehow, the room is even stranger in daylight. The furniture is positioned exactly how she remembers it from her childhood, but Miller has the odd sense that it's still not *quite* right, although she can't put her finger on how that is. Everything is approximately where it should be, but—perhaps things are slightly crooked, or pushed a few too many inches to the right, the distance misremembered by Sylvie as she'd arranged the furniture. The uncanny feeling isn't helped by the fact that Miller is older and bigger now, and that the cabin's bedroom is smaller than the one in her old home. It only lends itself to the feeling she has of being trapped in a child's doll house.

She sits in the quiet of her room, trying to ignore the sound of Sylvie bustling around the cabin. She can already smell the sausages frying in the pan and the sweetness of the beans in maple syrup on the stove. Sylvie had always liked having brunch on Saturdays, but Miller can't remember a time she had ever cooked it herself. It was always her dad—whenever he was home—grilling fatty meats and buttering toast while he burnt a full pan of scrambled eggs or forgot the hash browns in the oven for a little too long.

Miller's knees crack as she pushes herself up from the bed, body stiff and sore from the tiny paper-thin mattress with the worn box spring. She stretches her arms over her head, body shaking as she yawns, before she turns her attention toward getting dressed for the day.

Her duffel bag is open and waiting for her on the top of the armoire, but it's emptier than it should be. She picks it up and her heart sinks when she realises that all of her clothes have been taken out of the bag. She opens her bedroom door and pulls her housecoat tight as she makes her way to the kitchen. She doesn't look at the living room photos as she passes them.

"Morning, sweetie!" Sylvie calls from the kitchen when she hears Miller approaching.

"Sylvie, where's my clothing?" Miller asks, crossing her arms over her chest as she leans against the doorframe to the kitchen.

"Oh, I'm washing everything. It should be ready for the dryer soon."

"Why are you washing my clothes? They were clean. I didn't ask you to do that."

"I'm your mom, you don't need to ask me," Sylvie says in a singsong voice. A CD plays on the old sound system as she dances around the island, plating the food.

"Okay, but *why* did you wash my clothes without telling me? You shouldn't have done that without asking."

"Well," Sylvie picks her words carefully, "I didn't want to offend you by saying anything, *but* you kind of… you know… *stank of green* when I saw you yesterday. I smelled it this morning too when I came to your room to check on you while you were asleep. I could smell it coming from your bag, so I thought I'd do you a favour."

"Stank of green?" Miller asks, confused.

"You *know*."

"No, I don't, what are you talking about?"

Sylvie rolls her eyes and shakes her head, trying to look exasperated without actually being exasperated, putting this show on just for Miller.

"Weed, sweetie. You smelled like weed," she explains it like she's talking to a child. "Look, I know you care about her, but I wish that Florence would make better choices. I can't help but worry about the negative influence she's having on you—"

"You think she's a negative influence because she smokes?"

"Do you know how dangerous drugs are for a girl your age?"

"'A girl your age'? What am I, twelve?"

"Joke all you want, they can delay and stunt brain development, and don't get me started about what happens if you're high and go into work or get behind the wheel of a car!"

Sylvie's lecture on sobriety is funny to Miller, especially given that she grew up with her mother eagerly drinking her weight in wine even before her father's diagnosis.

"First of all, you know it's legal to smoke, yeah?"

"Just because it's legal, doesn't make it right And-"

"Secondly," Miller continues, "we don't smoke. We're doing our version of dry January, so we haven't smoked in a few weeks. So when you tell me that I smelled like weed, I can't help but think you're full of shit."

"If it wasn't you, and it wasn't Florence, then it was someone in your building who stunk it up for the rest of you. I was just trying to make sure my daughter had clean clothes for her weekend away."

"It was an invasion of my privacy."

"Why are you being so mean this morning?" Sylvie says, eyes watering. "I try to be kind and do some laundry for you, I cook you up your favourite breakfast, and you're so rude to me!"

Miller is stunned with Sylvie's version of events, but unsurprised by it. This is what it was like growing up with her: every event, every memory, rewritten and retold to you enough times that you couldn't help but wonder if the version you remembered was wrong. It always started with the tears she could summon on command, and ended with Miller apologising for something she never did and agreeing that Sylvie was right. Even now, Miller can't help but wonder if she's being too hard on Sylvie. She told Florence that she wanted to make it work with her mother, but the longer she's here, the less she believes it's true.

"I wasn't rude to you, Sylvie—"

"I'm just trying to protect you and take care of you, that's all."

"I appreciate it, but I'm an adult. I don't need you to—"

"I'm your mom. Of *course* I need to! But it feels like you're punishing my kindness!" she sobs.

"I'm sorry, I didn't mean to be ungrateful."

Sylvie sniffles and turns her attention to scrambling eggs, making sure they don't stick to the bottom of the pan. She wipes her eyes with the back of her hand before looking back at Miller with a big smile, her crocodile tears already dry.

"Could you move the plates a little closer?" she says, nodding towards the dishes on the island.

Miller nods in return and arranges the plates next to the stove for her mother. Instinctively, she starts buttering toast and scooping beans into small bowls while Sylvie plates the eggs, sausages, and hash browns. They dress their food at the island, in order to avoid cluttering the small surface of the kitchen table with jams and condiments, before taking their seats. They eat quietly, music the only sound filling the kitchen for some time. Miller doesn't have a lot to say to Sylvie, still frustrated at her intrusion, but after a few minutes of eating in near-silence, she tries to make conversation.

"It's really good."

"Thanks! I know it was your favourite, growing up."

Miller smiles and takes another bite, not wanting to admit that she'd never cared about breakfast food; she'd just loved getting to spend time with her dad after he'd been gone for so long.

"Can I get you anything else?" Sylvie asks, taking a sip of her orange juice.

"Actually, do we have any coffee? I'd kill for some, even the instant stuff."

Sylvie frowns. "You know that too much caffeine is bad for fertility, right?"

"Then it's a good thing I don't want kids."

"You know, I said that when I was your age. I was convinced I'd never want to be a mother and then, when I least expected it, I had you," Sylvie says with a warm smile.

Miller rolls her eyes internally. Her mother has changed the story about her conception so many times that she's convinced Sylvie has forgotten the truth of it herself. Thankfully, in a moment of lucidity, her father had once told her the truth: they'd planned meticulously for Miller's conception. He and Sylvie had tried for a baby for almost a year before she'd gotten pregnant, but she'd had a miscarriage at nearly five months. They'd tried again and, that time, lost the child after only three months, before finally getting pregnant with Miller and carrying her to term. According to her dad, the pregnancy hadn't been an easy one, and Sylvie had never gotten over the trauma of the miscarriages she'd had. Miller suspected her father hadn't gotten over it either.

"My perfect baby girl," Sylvie says, pulling Miller out of her thoughts. "So I wouldn't be so quick to say you don't want kids because, truthfully, you don't know what you want at that age."

"I'm thirty-four, not four, Sylvie. I know what I want at this age. I can tell you, with certainty, that kids aren't what I want."

Sylvie chuckles. "People change, Miller. That's all I'm saying. You might not want kids *now*, but next year? Or in five years? It might change. And it's lonely getting old by yourself. You'll want someone you love taking care of you, trust me.

Plus, you'll never understand the unconditional love that comes from being a mother. It's just—"

"I don't want kids, Sylvie. At all. Ever. And I won't be alone, I'll have Florence and whatever nurse we eventually hire. And, quite honestly, I think it says a lot about someone if they can't love another person unconditionally unless that person's their offspring. It's narcissistic."

Sylvie stares at Miller like she's been slapped. Her mouth hangs open and her eyes are dark as she looks her daughter up and down at the table, shaking her head.

"You're cruel, you know that?"

"I'm cruel?"

"It's bad enough that you're crushing my dreams of being a grandmother, of seeing your father's legacy continuing, but the way you talk to me? The things you say about me? They're just mean."

"I'm not being mean!"

"Yes you are. I was just trying to give you motherly advice and you treat me like shit every chance you get."

"You weren't giving me motherly advice, you were trying to invalidate my choice not to have kids. And this isn't the first time you've done this, either. I'm an adult, I know what I want, and I shouldn't have to prove that to you for you to respect my choices."

"I do respect your choices!" Sylvie says, aghast. "I didn't bat an eye when you first told me you were dating a woman! I might not like Florence or her lifestyle choices-"

"Her 'lifestyle choices'?" Miller asks, voice raised.

"—but I love you enough to support you and want to be there for you. All I was trying to do was tell you it's okay to change your mind! People do that! People change! They grow up and mature and—"

"There you go again, making it sound like I'm a kid who's not old enough to know what they want!" Miller yells.

"Don't raise your voice at me!"

"Then don't treat me like a child, Sylvie!"

"I told you to stop calling me that! It's 'Mom' to you!" she yells, slamming her hands down on the small table, the dishes rattling.

I wish it had been—

"I should have stayed home," Miller says calmly. "I knew this was a bad idea when you suggested it. I should have listened to my gut."

"You never wanted this to work, did you?" Sylvie asks quietly. "You were just doing this so you could pretend like you tried and have an excuse to keep me out of your life."

"Of course I wanted it to work. That's so not fair of you to say."

"You always do this. You take everything I say and you twist it and turn it against me. You always make me out to be some kind of monster when all I'm trying to do is keep our family together. Just, desperately, trying to make it work for the three of us."

'The three of us.'

Miller had never heard her mother refer to Florence as family and it catches her by surprise. She'd always assumed Sylvie still hated Florence for taking Miller away from her. When they'd started dating, Sylvie had mourned her time with (and control over) her daughter. The more Miller got away from home, the more she'd been able to realise how toxic it had grown to be after her father had gotten sick. Or maybe it had always been that way, with Sylvie holding on too tightly to the child that had survived, and she'd only noticed it when her father was no longer around to keep the household balanced.

It's a big step for Sylvie to call Florence anything other than the woman who stole her daughter, and Miller's stomach is suddenly in knots. Maybe she'd been too harsh with Sylvie, lording expectations over the woman that she could never meet. After all, it isn't just Sylvie who has work to do. Miller has been telling herself that Sylvie needs to change, but maybe it's Miller who needs to learn to accept her mother for who she is.

"I'm sorry," Miller finally says. "You're right. I'm not giving you a fair chance."

"No, you're not."

"I'll try harder."

"That's all I want, sweetie. That's all I've ever wanted."

The two of them finish their meal in silence before putting the dishes in the sink. Miller offers to wash them, but Sylvie insists she's happy to do it herself, even though Miller knows otherwise. While her mother's cleaning, Miller goes to the entranceway and unlocks the front door. She's tempted to pull her coat on over her pyjamas, but elects to leave the heavy parka hanging up on the hook and opens the door in just her housecoat, bracing herself for the frigid air.

Although the cold is exactly as harsh as she was expecting, what does manage to catch her off guard is how much snow has fallen overnight. While they'd gotten a nonstop dusting throughout the day on Friday, it seems like an ever bigger torrent of snow fell while they were asleep. The stairs desperately need shovelling and the path down to the Yaris is high with snow. The sun is bright overhead, but snow continues to fall and the sky looks dark on the horizon.

"Have you seen the snow yet?" Miller calls out to her mom.

"Yes! It's gorgeous, isn't it?"

"Yeah, uh—"

"I was thinking we could go snowshoeing before it gets too bad out there. It's supposed to storm all afternoon, so I doubt we'll have sun for too much longer."

"Yeah, it looks like it's going to get bad fast."

"Which is why we should take advantage of the sun while we can!" Sylvie says cheerfully.

Miller closes the door and heads back to the kitchen, rubbing her hands together quickly to warm them from the cold.

"Look, I hate suggesting this, but maybe we should postpone our weekend and use today to get home."

"I thought you said you were going to try?"

"I am, I swear I am. You can pick any weekend this month or whenever and we'll come back out here, but I'm worried that the snow's going to get bad out here with the storm. We're alone in the middle of nowhere and I think there's a whiteout headed to our door. It might just be safer for us to leave and—"

Sylvie shakes her head, obviously not willing to hear another word on the subject. "It just looks bad, but it's going to be fine. There's a backup generator in case the power goes out and we're not *too* far from other people in case something goes south. It'll be fine. You need to stop worrying."

"Sylvie, I'm serious, I think—"

"It's 'Mom,'" she insists. "And we're staying. It's going to be fine."

Miller disagrees, but keeps quiet in light of the fight they had only moments ago.

"Okay."

"Okay," Sylvie repeats. "So we'll go snowshoeing and then maybe we can play some board games when we get back?"

"Yeah, that sounds nice."

"Great! So get changed—your stuff is in the dryer—and we'll head out."

Miller nods and heads upstairs, slippers quiet on the hardwood, to check on her clothing in the machines in the spare room. As worried as she is about the storm, she's more worried about keeping the peace with Sylvie, and so she keeps the rest of her concerns to herself. She's not sure if it's the adrenaline from the argument or if it's something else, but she feels more anxious than normal and is eager to go home.

Just one more day, she thinks, mentally counting down the hours between now and tomorrow afternoon.

She passes by her mother's bedroom, the sour smell still lingering by the door. She grimaces at the acidity of the aroma, surprised that she forgot to mention it to Sylvie earlier. Curious to know where it's coming from, she tries to turn the cold metal handle and pushes the door with her shoulder, but the wooden door doesn't budge. She tries again, but realises that it's not just the wood that's immobile but the handle that's stiff too: it's locked. She takes another sniff, trying to figure out what the smell is, her nose wrinkling as she breathes in. Finally, unable to place the scent, she turns back to the spare room and pushes her way through the boxes to the ancient machines.

She smiles to herself, recognizing the appliances from the basement of her childhood home, and opens the dryer.

Nothing's in there.

Frowning, Miller turns her attention to the top-loading washer, the lid weighted down by a bottle of detergent and a bottle of bleach. She moves the soap onto the top of the dryer, glad that this is at least new and not a remnant from her childhood. She picks up the bleach and frowns at how wet it is, streaks of the chemical trailing down the bottle and making a ring of liquid on top of the machine. She looks for some paper towels to wipe everything up but, finding none, she puts the bottle down next to the detergent and hopes the liquid doesn't dribble into the machine when she lifts the lid.

Opening the washer, she finds her clothing still soaking wet—as though the final spin was interrupted—and discoloured, like bleach has already been poured into the machine. Upon closer inspection, some of her garments are ripped, cleanly torn like they've been shredded with scissors.

"What the fuck?"

She pulls item after item out of the drum, boiling over with anger as each piece of clothing she removes is spotted with bleach and torn to strips. She throws everything back into the machine and slams the lid closed before storming downstairs.

"Did you find them?" Sylvie asks, putting the last of the pans in the dish rack.

"Yeah, I found them."

"Good! So go get ready, you're wasting daylight!"

"I can't get ready, you fucking ruined everything."

"What do you mean?" she asks, blank expression plastered on her face.

"Don't play dumb, Sylvie. It's fucked. Everything is ripped to shreds and covered in bleach."

"I don't understand."

"What word gave you trouble?" Miller snaps.

"Sweetie, I threw your laundry in with some detergent earlier this morning and I'm pretty sure I put everything in the dryer too, but it's possible I forgot when I was making breakfast for us."

"Did you also remember to run everything through a blender too?"

Sylvie only stares at her blankly, so Miller grabs her by the arm and pulls her up the stairs. When she gets to the machine, she opens the lid and holds up her jeans, which more closely resemble a makeshift rag than a pair of pants.

"Oh God," Sylvie says. "What *happened*?"

Miller squints at Sylvie, trying to gauge her reaction. It could be her frustration with the situation, but she can't help but think her mother's eyes are open a little *too* wide, her voice a little *too* high.

"You tell me."

"Miller, all I did was put your laundry in, pour some soap in with everything, and put it on a normal cycle."

"So the bleach just… ?" she asks, shaking her head.

"I really don't know what to tell you. Maybe it was left over in the machine from the last load of whites I did?"

"Sylvie, the side of the damned bottle's still wet!" Miller exclaims.

Her mom frowns and reaches out to feel the bottle, only instead of grabbing the bleach she feels her way along the side of the detergent.

"I don't feel any—"

"That's the detergent, Sylvie."

"What?"

"You're touching the detergent. The bleach is in the other bottle."

"Oh," she picks up the white bottle and squints at it, turning it over in her hands. "OH!" Sylvie finally shouts. Miller can't help but think it looks more like a pantomime of horror than sincere concern. "I'm so sorry, Miller, I accidentally put this in thinking it was the detergent."

"You couldn't tell that the white bottle that looks like bleach wasn't the bright orange bottle of soap?"

"I don't know what to say, I think I was just too distracted. I'm really sorry, Miller. It was an honest mistake."

"And did you pour it in before or after putting my stuff through a paper shredder?"

"I didn't run your clothes through a shredder, Miller," Sylvie dismisses. "Don't be so dramatic. You know how old washers are."

Miller stares at her mother in disbelief. "You know, that you mention it, no. I don't think I do."

"Sometimes the agitator breaks and clothes get ripped while they're getting washed. And if your things had holes already, then the machine could have easily made them worse."

"There's no way that's true."

"A hundred percent, it is," Sylvie says, crossing her arms over her chest.

Miller knows her mother's lying. Having grown up hearing her mothers lies, half-truths, and skewed versions of events, Miller knows when something Sylvie says doesn't ring true. And yet… Miller can't imagine why Sylvie would go to such lengths to intentionally destroy her clothing. She easily admitted to taking her belongings and putting them in the washer, so why Sylvie would purposefully destroy her clothing when Miller knows she was the last person to touch it is beyond her. It doesn't add up at all.

"Well, I don't know what to tell you, but I don't think I'll be able to go snowshoeing," Miller says with an exasperated sigh. "Strangely, I'm not in the mood to roam the woods in my PJs."

Sylvie smiles calmly. "You won't have to. Check your dresser when you get to your room. There should be some spare clothes in there."

"Fine."

Although Miller and Sylvie are roughly the same size, she's not especially grateful for this fact right now, although she doesn't share that thought with her mother. She also doesn't tell Sylvie that she wants to go home now more than ever. Between the unending snow and the fast-approaching storm, this cabin is the last place she wants to be.

She turns on her heel and exits the spare room, passing her mother's door on the way to the stairs. She stops the second the smell hits her and she points to the bedroom door as her mom exits the spare room.

"Why does your room stink so much?"

"What?"

"Your room, there's a smell coming from it."

"No there isn't."

Miller frowns. "Yes, there is. It's gross."

"Well, I don't smell anything, so I wouldn't worry about it."

"Sylvie, it smells awful. You really can't smell it?"

Her mother stops and halfheartedly sniffs the air. "I mean, now that you mention it, I guess there's something a little funky."

"It's disgusting. It smells like death."

"I don't know, sweetie, maybe a raccoon died in the wall."

"Ew. Shouldn't we look for it and get rid of it?"

Her mother shrugs, and Miller is surprised by Sylvie's uncharacteristically casual handling of the situation. "We'll find it eventually."

"*You'll* find it eventually. I'm only here until tomorrow."

Sylvie frowns, suddenly looking upset. "Just get dressed so we can go, okay?"

Miller nods and heads back downstairs to her room. Although she's deeply unexcited about the prospect of dressing like her mother—who unironically dresses like it's still 1995—she's excited to get out of her sleepwear and get on with her weekend. She closes the door to her room behind her, throws the housecoat on the unmade bed, and opens the top drawer of the dresser.

Her heart stops. She closes the drawer.

She opens the next drawer, a pit forming in her stomach as she examines its contents.

It's not her mother's spare clothes in the dresser. It's not even the clothing she left behind when she moved out with Florence after college.

It's the same clothing she wore when she was just a kid, only bigger.

She picks up a pair of blue jeans and looks them over. They're big enough to fit her, but they look like they could be made for a child, with bright pink flowers and white daisies embroidered down the side. They look like a pair she used to own when she was in kindergarten, only these ones have been hand stitched, the flowers clumsy and uneven. She riffles through the t-shirts, finding a collection of Disney princesses silk screened on Fruit of the Loom v-necks and likely thrifted at a Value Village. Even the socks and underwear that have been folded carefully leave her uneasy, with bright colours and childish patterns she's much too old to wear.

Miller gets dressed and looks at herself in the mirror. For a moment, she feels like she's not looking at herself, and is instead staring into one of the old family portraits hanging in the other room. The illusion is only broken when her mother calls to her from the kitchen, warning her that they're wasting daylight.

Before she leaves her bedroom, Miller types up a text to Florence and hits send, already knowing it won't go through.

Come get me. NOW.

SATURDAY, JANUARY 15, 12:06 P.M.

Even with the snowshoes on, Miller is struggling. On the one hand, she appreciates being outside, getting a break from the cabin; on the other, she's having difficulty navigating the narrow paths crowded with trees that grab at her jacket and the snow drifts that appear out of nowhere and block her way. She and Sylvie are moving through a clearing, slowly making their way to the forest path on the other side. Miller stops and looks up at the bright sky overhead. She pulls her scarf down to enjoy the feeling of the sun on her face, even as the wind bites at her exposed skin. While she's enjoying the daylight, Miller can't help but notice that the clouds have gotten darker since they left. There's no denying that a massive storm is coming.

"Isn't it a beautiful day out today?" Sylvie asks.

"Yeah, gorgeous. But the clouds—"

"Oh, don't worry about them. We'll be safe in the cabin."

The cabin.

She doesn't want to go back there. She wants to go home. As nervous as she is at the thought of driving through a whiteout, the idea of staying another minute leaves her feeling uneasy. Between the old furnishings, her mom's unusual behaviour, and the clothing that was chosen for her, her mind once again returns to the image of herself as a doll trapped in a dollhouse.

When she'd confronted Sylvie about the clothing that had been left in the dresser for her, her mom had seemed confused by Miller's discomfort.

"But you used to *love* wearing clothing like this," she'd said, eyes watering as she took in Miller in her floral jeans and bright pink sweater.

"Yeah, when I was a child, Sylvie."

"I don't understand, you don't like wearing jeans or warm clothes now? You're too cool for them?"

"No, it's not that, it's just—"

"So then why are you complaining? Besides, you look so cute like this! My little girl!" she'd practically sobbed before ushering Miller to get her coat on and stop "burning daylight."

Even the snowshoes and poles she'd been given to use by Sylvie looked… wrong. They were the standard kind she'd been using for most of her life: lightweight aluminium with polypropylene and steel cleats. But instead of being a solid colour, these were painted bright pink and blue with a matching floral pattern on the poles. While it didn't bother her to use brightly coloured gear—she was borrowing it from Sylvie, after all—it did bother her that Sylvie had gone out of her way to find this *specific* equipment for her ahead of time.

Even her winter accessories had been selected with bright colours and childish patterns in mind. Sylvie had insisted that Miller ditch her old scarf, hat, and gloves in exchange for the baby blue and cotton candy pink set she'd knit for her. Although Miller had insisted on just wearing the gear she'd brought with her, she'd quickly discovered that they'd gone missing from the basket by the door.

"Ready to keep going?" Sylvie asks, kicking her left leg a few times to shake some of the snow off her snowshoe.

"Yeah, I'm good," Miller replies, pulling her scarf over her nose.

The two of them continue through the woods, taking turns breaking trail. As much as Miller doesn't want to be alone in the mountains with her mom, she can't help but enjoy stepping through fresh powder and crushing it flat with her snowshoes. In the city, people walk the few available trails at all hours of the day, which end up so well travelled that you hardly need boots, let alone snowshoes. She misses spending time in the wild like this, like she did when she was younger.

Her father used to take her ice fishing, skiing, and snowshoeing when she was a kid. Sylvie would always stay home, not wanting to spend the day sweating in heavy layers. When Miller and her dad would finally come in, there'd be hot chocolate ready with marshmallows and a roast would be in the oven for dinner. These are some of the few memories of her mother that she looks back on fondly.

She stops near a tree, checking to make sure that the upper branches aren't dangerously heavy with snow, before unclipping the water bottle from her belt and taking a swig.

"Doing okay?" Sylvie asks.

"Yeah, just tired. I haven't walked this much in a long time."

"I can tell!" Sylvie chuckles. "You're bigger than I remember!"

"Fucking what?" Miller asks, stunned.

"Oh, sweetie, I'm not saying you're *fat* or anything," she says, whispering 'fat' like it's a slur, "but I can't help but notice that you've put on a few pounds since you started seeing Florence."

"I have, but I'm so confused as to why you thought it was okay to comment on it."

"I'm your mom, sweetie. If I don't tell you the hard truths then no one will. I'm just trying to look out for you. But don't worry, we're having a healthy, low-calorie dinner tonight. So it won't wreck your diet."

"I'm not on a diet," Miller drawls, hooking the bottle onto her belt and continuing along the wooded path. "I haven't been on one since the diet you had me on as a kid."

"Okay, well it won't wreck your 'lifestyle change' or whatever you call it."

"Can we stop talking about my body?"

"No need to be so sensitive, Miller. I'm just trying to look out for you. You're my little girl, after all."

"Wow, does this ever bring back memories," Miller says, exhaling slowly through her mouth as she tries to calm herself down.

"Oh yeah?" Sylvie asks pleasantly. "Like what?"

"Like being told I was too fat to go to birthday parties because you worried I'd eat too much and gain weight," Miller snaps.

"Oh, come on, you had no self-control—"

"Or how you'd put me on those cleanses, where I'd drink cayenne pepper and lemon juice all fucking day because you didn't think I was skinny enough to eat real food."

Sylvie crosses her arms over her chest, the ski poles clanging together as she watches Miller, unamused.

"You can get as mad at me as you want," Sylvie says, "but you *know* what I did was only to help you. And it looks like it worked, too, you skinny minny!"

Miller makes a face, like she's eating lemons, and shakes her head. "You fucked me up for a long time. And I mean a *long* time."

"Why are you bringing this up now?" Sylvie asks. "Did you hate the idea of us enjoying *one* afternoon together so much that you had to start a fight?"

"*Me*?" Miller shouts. "You're the one who felt the need to say something about my weight!"

"I'm your mother! I'm allowed to be worried about you!"

I wish it had been—

"Whatever. Let's just go."

They walk in silence, heading back to the cabin as the snow blows harder. The flakes of white come down harder and faster now, the sky overhead growing darker by the minute.

"How far is the cabin?" Miller asks.

"Not too far! What games did you want to play when we get back?"

"I think I'm going to take some time for myself, actually."

"Oh, well maybe we can watch a movie on the old VHS player. I think I still have some of your—"

"I think I just want to be alone for a bit."

Sylvie is silent as Miller continues to push forward, breaking trail and hoping the cabin is close. She's tired of hiking through the woods, the snow getting deeper each second, and she desperately wants to call Florence to come get her. She knows the text she sent before heading out likely didn't get delivered, but she wishes with every part of her heart that it did.

"Why do you hate me so much?" Sylvie finally asks.

Miller doesn't want to answer. She's worried that if she starts listing the reasons, she won't be able to stop.

"I asked you a question," her mother pushes.

"I don't hate you. I never said I hated you," Miller finally snaps. "But I'm tired of you acting like we're friends. Like we're close. Like I had a picture-perfect childhood where everything was happy and easy and good. I didn't. It wasn't."

"How can you even say that? You had a great childhood. Your father loved you more than anything in the world and I love you just as much!" Sylvie shouts.

"I know Dad loved me. I never once doubted that Dad loved me."

"But you don't think I do?" her mother asks, strangled.

"I didn't say that."

"No, you implied it."

"No, I didn't!"

"You said that—"

"I'm just saying that while Dad *and* you loved me, Dad's the only one who ever made me feel like he meant it. I think you think you were a great mom, but you were selfish and you were mean and you made everything about you. Why the fuck do you think I cut you out? For fun?"

Sylvie looks like she's been slapped. Her face is twisted with anger and hurt and Miller can't help but regret her words, even if they're true. She doesn't want to make things worse, but she also can't help but think that they'll never fix what's between them. Maybe it would be better if they tore everything down and built their relationship from scratch.

"I think it's just incredible how you can look at everything around you, everything I've done for you, and piss all over it," Sylvie finally says, making her way up the trail ahead of Miller. "I can't believe you think so little about me that you feel like I was a terrible mother who didn't love you."

"That isn't what I said!" Miller shouts.

"That's exactly what you said!" Sylvie screams back.

"You're not fucking listening to me, Sylvie!"

"I told you to call me 'Mom'!" Sylvie shrieks, shoving her daughter with all her strength.

Miller is already slipping before she has time to process what's happened. She swings and stabs her poles at the ground, trying to catch herself, but is unable to find purchase. She tries to step backwards, but the heels of the shoes—which are only meant to go forward—drag against the ground and trip her up worse. As she struggles to find her balance, Miller accidentally catches herself on an icy patch of ground and is soon flying backwards down the hill. She tumbles through the snow, poles flying and snowshoes unlatching, as she falls uncontrollably, her body eventually stopping its descent when she crashes face-first into a tree.

"Miller!" her mother screams, running after her as carefully as she can, trying to cut herself a path down the slope without striking ice.

Miller pushes herself off of the rough bark, warm blood filling her mouth and spilling over her chin. She sits back in the snow, which quickly turns red around her as she hunches forward and tries to catch her breath. The wind has been knocked out of her and everything hurts. She gasps for air between shaky sobs. Her face is aching and, if she had to guess, her nose has been broken or badly bruised. Her lip is split—she can feel the air hitting the cut—and her cheek feels raw and scratched. Her hands are sore from the impact against the tree, but thankfully none of her fingers seem to be broken.

Sylvie is still making her way down the hill. As Miller's breathing starts to return to normal, she tries standing up. The second she puts weight onto her left leg, she feels like she's going to throw up. She sits back down and feels her leg over her snow pants. Her leg feels fine until she gets to her knee, which throbs at even the lightest touch and already feels swollen through the thick fabric. Miller's sure she's sprained it, if not worse.

"Oh God, Miller!" her mom cries out when she sees her face. "I'm so sorry. I didn't mean to do that. I just, I lost my temper and I don't know what came over me. Oh, sweetie, I'm so *so* sorry."

"What the fuck is wrong with you?" Miller gasps furiously.

"I didn't mean to! You know I'm never angry like this!"

Sylvie begins to cry as she falls to her knees next to Miller in the snow. Each heave is loud and exaggerated and her nose begins to run. She reaches a hand out and touches Miller's bloody face, before her daughter slaps it away.

"Ow! That fucking hurts!" Miller shouts, lip stinging.

"I'm just trying to help!"

"Well don't!"

"Fine!" Sylvie shouts, standing up and glowering over Miller. "You don't want my help? Fine. *Fine*. You're welcome to make your way back to the cabin without me then!"

Miller looks at the long path ahead of her and the black clouds hanging low in the sky. The idea of trying to find her way back to the cabin when the whiteout hits sends a shiver of fear through her. As furious as she is with Sylvie, she realises now's not the time to hold a grudge.

I wish it had been—

"I'm sorry," Miller says. "It's just, it hurt when you touched it."

"Well it's not like I meant to hurt you!" she weeps.

“No, I know. I’m sorry.”

“I didn’t mean to push you.”

“I know you didn’t. It’s okay. Everything’s going to be okay,” Miller says, comforting her mother through a mouthful of blood that she spits into the red snow. “I didn’t mean to be so rude.”

“Don’t worry about it,” Sylvie says, extending a hand. "I forgive you."

Miller takes her hand before Sylvie can have a change of heart, and her mother helps her to her feet. She leans on Sylvie, unable to put any weight on her left leg, and together they make their way back to the cabin.

SATURDAY, JANUARY 15, 3:12 P.M.

The sky is black by the time Miller and Sylvie get back to the cabin, the snow whipping around them in a fury of white. Miller's face feels like it's on fire, the wind stinging her skin and open wounds, and she's never been more grateful to see the old wooden building. Sylvie helps Miller up the steps, huffing in annoyance every time her daughter needs a break, before unlocking the front door with a silver key, which she slips under her snow pants and into her back pocket, before pushing the door open and leading Miller onto the living room couch.

"Do you need help taking off your things?" Sylvie asks.

"No, I think I'm—ow!" Miller yells as Sylvie pulls off her daughter's boots.

"Sorry!" Sylvie says loudly, moving the wet boots to the entranceway and getting a paper towel from the kitchen. "I didn't want to get the floors wet. You have no idea how expensive it is to repair hardwood flooring."

Miller cradles her sore knee, which is once again throbbing from the careless way Sylvie had ripped off her footwear. Once she's no longer seeing spots, she pulls her hat and gloves off before lowering her scarf from over her nose, the wool sticking to the near-frozen blood on her face. She goes to toss everything onto the floor, but Sylvie is beside her with a garbage bag before she can let go of the clothing.

"Here. Put everything you need to wash in here," she says, motioning to Miller's jacket.

Miller doesn't bother arguing and, instead, follows Sylvie's instructions. She unzips her heavy coat and leans forward, shrugging it off her back.

"You're not going to throw it all out, right?"

"No, of course not. I'm going to go wash it once mine's done. You dripped all over me on the way back," she accuses, dropping the garbage bag onto the ground beside the couch and heading to the bathroom.

"Uh, sorry. How careless of me, I guess."

Miller lifts her hips, putting all of her weight on her right leg as she wiggles her snow pants down off her waist. Once they're down to her knees, she sits normally and pulls them the rest of the way off, taking extra care to remove them gently from her sore leg before throwing them into the garbage bag with the rest of her outerwear.

She stares at her leg and knows that something is seriously wrong with it. The jeans around her left knee are tight and stiff, the joint having swollen to a massive size. She closes her eyes and breathes in through her mouth, still unable to breathe through her nose. She holds the breath for a count of four, before slowly emptying it out again through her mouth. The pain is all-consuming and it takes everything in her not to cry.

The walk back to the cabin was hard on Miller. Although it should have been a thirty-minute hike from where they were under normal conditions, it had taken the two of them the better part of two hours to get in. Between the breaks she'd needed, the increasingly heavy snowfall, and the fact that her poles and snowshoes had gotten lost in the fall, Miller was almost impressed that it had *only* taken them two hours.

"Do you want some Advil, sweetie? Tylenol?"

"Yes, please."

"Which one?"

"Both."

"You can't take both, it'll kill you."

"No, you can take both at the same time. They're different medications."

Sylvie comes back with a small cup of water and two Advil. "I don't want you making things worse," she says in response to Miller's questioning look when she notices the missing Tylenol.

"Whatever."

She swallows the pills down with the water, cringing from the pain of the cold glass against her sore lip. She breathes through her mouth and tries to stay calm as she looks at her knee straining against her denim pants. Like she did with her snow pants, Miller thrusts her hips forward and begins sliding the pants down her legs, needing to get herself out of the constricting fabric. Unfortunately, when she gets to the swollen joint, the pants are practically immovable as the tight fabric is held in place by her too-large knee.

"I need scissors," Miller calls out to her mom.

"For what?"

"I need to get these pants off and they're stuck."

Sylvie comes back to the living room carrying a wet washcloth, which she places on the denim.

"You don't need to cut them off, you just need to wet the fibres enough so that they'll stretch over it."

Miller is skeptical about her mother's approach, but she holds her tongue and waits as the cloth soaks the jeans around her knee. She then grabs the bottom hem of the pant leg and pulls slowly, the fabric still too tight around Miller's leg.

"Ah! Stop," she says, grabbing at Sylvie's hands. "It really hurts. I think it's too tight to slip over."

Sylvie frowns, shaking her head. "You're just being a baby," she tells Miller as she holds on tighter to the fabric and yanks.

Miller screams and folds forward, holding her leg. "Stop! Just stop! Please, *please*, just go get the scissors."

"But I worked so hard on these!" Sylvie complains, getting up from the couch. Instead of going to get the scissors, she moves across the living room, stopping in front of a photo and placing her hand against the glass. "I wanted to make them special for you."

"They are," Miller says desperately, "I really love them. I hope you can make me another pair after we cut these off."

"But maybe we don't have to cut them off!" Sylvie says, coming back to the couch and grabbing hold of Miller's jeans once more.

"Yes," she shouts, trying to shoo her mom away, "we do! Please, I'm begging you, just get the scissors."

Reluctantly, Sylvie lets go and leaves the room, returning with a pair of scissors that she hands over to Miller handle-first.

"I need you to cut them for me," Miller says. "I can't reach properly with my leg extended."

Sylvie seems heartbroken at having to mangle the pants herself, but she does as Miller says. She cuts through the bottom hem and slowly slides the scissors up the leg, making sure not to accidentally stick or catch her daughter's skin on the bottom blade.

"Okay, that should be good enough," Miller tells Sylvie when the cut has reached mid-shin. She leans forward, grabs the fabric with both hands and begins to pull it apart. The denim rips and splits, albeit not easily, but soon Miller's made the hole big enough for her to pull her knee through.

She looks at the joint and grimaces at the sight. The skin is bright red and both the front and back of the knee are swollen beyond belief. It hurts to even look at it, let alone move it, and Miller goes back to slowly breathing through her mouth in an attempt to calm herself down.

"This isn't good," she tells Sylvie. "I really think I need to get to a hospital."

"In *this* weather?" Sylvie asks, appalled.

Miller turns her attention to the snow falling outside the window. If she thought the storm was bad before, it's nothing compared to how it looks now. The wind rattles the glass panes, which look like they've been painted white.

Through the snow, Miller can make out a few shadows that look like trees bent in half from the force of the storm. Even the cabin seems to have noticed how bad it's gotten, the lights beginning to flicker.

"Do you think the power's going to go out?"

Sylvie shrugs, nonplussed. "If it does, like I said, we have a backup generator. I wouldn't worry about it too much. I made sure this place could run all on its own."

"Maybe we should call an ambulance."

"Why?"

"For my leg. I mean, we obviously shouldn't drive when it's like this, but I don't think it's a good idea for me to stay. And I don't even know how my face looks. Maybe we should—"

"Your face looks fine," Sylvie interrupts, "and I'm sure your leg will be okay."

"I can't put any pressure on it. At all."

"That's normal when you injure something. Just make sure to ice it for the next few days—that shouldn't be too hard thanks to the weather—then apply heat and you'll be golden."

"It looks really bad. I *really* think I should see a doctor."

"You are. You're seeing Doctor Mom," she laughs.

"I'm serious, Sylvie." Her mother's eye twitches at the sound of her name, "I think I need to go."

"No!" Sylvie shouts. "I didn't put in all this work, go through all this effort, work *so hard* for you to ruin it! You're fine! You don't need to leave because nothing is wrong! We're going to be a family again! Okay? The three of us are going to be a family and it's going to be good and you're okay! OKAY?"

Miller stares at her mother, her chest tight with panic. She breathes fast through her mouth and, for the first time in her life, she's truly afraid of Sylvie and what she might do. She's seen her mother in a rage before, she's even seen her mother violent before, but never has she seen her mother quite so desperate to hold on.

Sylvie stares at Miller expectantly.

"Yeah. Yeah, of course," she finally tells her mother, mouth dry. "I'm not going anywhere."

I can't, even if I wanted to, she thinks.

Sylvie smiles and heads back into the kitchen. "How about a hot chocolate, kiddo?" she asks. From the other room, Miller can hear her mom fill up the kettle and put it down on the stove.

"Uh, actually, I think I'm going to grab a shower. The water might feel good on my leg," she lies. She doesn't tell Sylvie that what she really wants is to get her phone and call for help. She doesn't tell Sylvie that she just desperately wants to leave.

"Sounds good, sweetie. I'll make it when you get out," her mother calls from the other room. "But don't be too long in the shower; you need to ice your knee."

"Yeah, okay."

Miller holds onto the arm of the sofa as she stands up, putting all of the weight on her right leg. Her bedroom is just across the room and at the end of the hall, but with her knee it seems impossibly far away. She slowly tests her left leg, trying to put a bit of weight on it, and winces, her face crumpling in on itself.

"Here, let me help," Sylvie says, coming back from the other room. She extends a hand, but Miller waves her off.

"No, no, I'll be okay. I need to be able to do this on my own."

"No, you don't. I'm here for you. I'll always be here to take care of you."

Before Miller can protest again, Sylvie slides her arm around her and begins leading her to the bathroom. Reflexively, Miller leans on her mother and lets her help carry her to the washroom.

Once they're in the small room, Miller leans against the vanity as Sylvie turns on the tap of the shower.

"Oh, you don't have to do that for me."

Her mother smiles, seemingly ignoring her, holding the tips of her fingers under the running water as she sets the perfect temperature. Once she's satisfied, she dries her hand on her pants and moves towards Miller, grabbing the hem of her sweater and beginning to lift it up. Surprised and confused, Miller pushes her mother's hands away.

"What are you doing?" she asks, voice cracking.

"Helping you get into your shower."

"I can do it myself, thanks."

"Oh, nonsense, I don't mind helping you."

"No, I'm really okay," she argues, pulling her shirt down. She suddenly wishes she still had on her painfully tight jeans, her bare legs feeling exposed in a way they hadn't moments before.

"It's not like I haven't seen everything before," Sylvie laughs. "I used to change you. I used to bathe you!"

"Yeah, sure, but I also used to shit myself. We all grow out of things."

Her mother frowns. "Language," she says, shaking her head in disappointment. "Now let me help you."

"No," Miller says firmly. "If I need your help, you'll be the first one to know."

Sylvie goes quiet, looking unhappy, and Miller can't help but worry that she's going to lash out again. Instead, her mother leaves the bathroom silently and closes the door behind her. Miller reaches out to lock the door behind Sylvie, but realises with a start that there's no lock on the door.

In fact, now that she thinks about it, her mother's bedroom and the front door are the only ones with locks on them.

The thought unsettles her.

Miller tests her leg on the tiled floor, bracing herself against the bathroom counter as she slowly puts weight on her left leg. The pain is excruciating and she starts to see spots in her vision. She wants nothing more than to sneak back down the hallway, grab her cell phone, and call for help, but she doubts that's an option anymore thanks to her knee. She tries walking to the tub without holding onto the counter. It's painful, slow, and she nearly falls face-first into the wall.

Her face.

She realises with a start that she hasn't looked at herself since the collision with the tree. Her heart beats faster at the idea of seeing herself. She knows that the mystery of what her injuries look like must be worse than the truth of what's happened to her, so she turns—mindful not to rotate her knee too much—and faces her reflection.

Her heart stops.

She was wrong.

She looks *much* worse than she was expecting.

Her eyes are bruised, dark rings like the markings of a raccoon frame her eyes; only, instead of black, they're a grisly mess of blue, purple, and bright red. Miller's nose is no better: a deep cut crosses the thickly bruised bridge, and it's swollen to twice its normal size. It also leans to the left, something it never used to do. Dried blood rings her nostrils and stains a trail down her face that mixes with the blood from her mouth. The gash on her lip is gruesome and deep, cutting clean through the pink tissue and stopping short of her chin. No wonder it hurts to talk. Even her cheek, which she thought she'd only just scraped, looks like it lost a battle with a cheese grater.

Between her face and her leg, Miller's sure she needs a doctor. How she's going to get there is another question entirely.

"Everything going okay, sweetie?" her mother calls to her through the door.

"Fine! Thanks for asking!"

"Alrighty, well shout if you need anything!"

Miller listens to Sylvie's footsteps fade away before she takes off her sweater, stretching the neck as wide as she can as she pulls it over her head, the fabric dragging against her broken nose, before repeating the same process with her t-shirt. She then takes off the rest of her undergarments—she needs to sit on the toilet to take her socks off, her left leg having nearly buckled when she tried holding herself up to peel off the right sock—and climbs into the shower, clinging to the tiled wall as she lifts her leg over the ledge of the bathtub.

The water feels good on her body, but the flecks of moisture that land on her face sting her sore skin. There's a small fog-proof mirror mounted on the shampoo rack in the tub which she uses to guide her hands as she washes the blood off her face. She tries to get it all, but doesn't quite manage; it hurts too much to keep trying. She washes her hair with the cheap shampoo her mother's used her whole life and washes her body down with an equally cheap bar of soap. When she's done, she's surprisingly tired from all the effort and she just wants to lie down.

She reaches for one of the towels hanging on the wall, but her hand doesn't find one. When she opens the curtains to look, thinking her memory of the bathroom's setup must be off, she's startled to find that the towel rack is empty.

"Hey, can I please have a towel?" Miller calls from behind the curtain, hoping her mother can hear her from the other room.

She doesn't have to worry, though, as Sylvie opens the door almost as soon as the question is asked, like she's been waiting for her.

"I've got one here for you, sweetie," she beams.

Miller reaches out for the towel but Sylvie doesn't hand it over. Instead, she holds open the massive towel and approaches the shower, pushing the curtain wide open with an elbow.

"What the fuck?!" Miller shouts, trying to cover herself with her hands while also trying to hold onto the wall for support.

"I'm going to dry you off, silly."

Sylvie moves forward with the towel, a corner of the cotton fabric in each hand, and tries to give Miller a bear hug with it. Sylvie engulfs her in the fabric and starts trying to pat her wet skin down. Miller pushes her off, wincing in pain as she shoves her mother back.

"Stop it!" she yells, shivering in the cold of the open door as she leans against the wet tiles. "This is so fucking weird, Sylvie! Just give me the towel and get out!"

Sylvie stares at her daughter, her mouth opening and closing what seems like a hundred times before turning into a furious snarl.

"How many times do I have to tell you to call me 'Mom'? HOW MANY?" Sylvie screams. "I'm tired of you disrespecting me like this in my own home! Wait until he hears about this, young lady, he's going to be so disappointed in you. SO DISAPPOINTED!"

"What the hell are you talking about? WHO's going to be disappointed in me, Sylvie?" she asks, her mother's name slipping from her lips.

Sylvie screams wordlessly and drops the towel before reaching across the tub and slapping Miller across the face. The force slams her head against the shower tile, her broken face jostling from the blow. She shouts in pain, but Sylvie doesn't care. Instead, she grabs Miller by the ear and pulls it hard, forcing her daughter to hobble after her on her bad leg. Miller cries from the agony of it, trying to find her footing as she slips on the hardwood floors made wet from her naked body, and she clings to the walls of the hallway for support as Sylvie drags her to her room.

"You're grounded until dinner," she tells Miller, letting go of her daughter's ear once she crosses the threshold of her bedroom.

Miller falls to the ground and hugs her leg to her chest, breathing hard through her sobs of pain.

I wish it had been—

"I want you to *really* think about how you use your words, how you hurt me with them, and think very carefully about how you're going to speak to me moving forward." Sylvie grabs Miller's phone from her bedside table and waves it in front of her. "You'll get this back when you learn some respect."

She leaves the room, slamming the door closed behind her as Miller cries on the floor. From the hallway, she hears the faint metal click of a bolt sliding into place.

It seems Miller had been wrong about the locks.

Her door has one. It's just on the other side.

SATURDAY, JANUARY 15, 4:33 P.M.

Miller sits on the floor for a long time, holding her knee. Although she hadn't twisted it on the way down the hall, putting her full weight on the leg and stumbling over hardwood has made both the pain and swelling worse.

Now, it's almost the size of a honeydew melon.

By the time she's finally calmed down enough to try and stand up, she's shivering so hard it feels like her body's convulsing, and her hair is no longer dripping wet. Getting up off of the floor is a slow and arduous process, and getting across the room to her dresser is an even longer one. She uses furniture and the walls to support her weight, making sure she's fully supported before taking each step.

Once she reaches her dresser, she tries putting on sweatpants before giving up and settling for a long-sleeved nightgown with cartoon cats and a pair of pink boxer shorts. The pants wouldn't fit comfortably over her leg and she's tired of touching it; every movement only makes her injury worse.

Once dressed, she focuses her attention on escaping the room. It's clear that Sylvie has become unhinged, and Miller isn't keen on sticking around for her to get more of her body bruised and broken. She tests the door, already knowing the effort is pointless, before focusing on the windows.

It's immediately clear that this is also a dead end.

Sylvie's nailed her windows shut from the outside.

She hadn't noticed the metal driven through the wooden frames when she'd first seen her room—she was too distracted by the memories of her old home—but now it's all she notices. She tries to wiggle the windows up, but she can tell this is a lost cause. She then tries pushing against the wooden muntin bar, trying to raise the window from there, but all it does is hurt her fingers. To Miller, these windows might as well be solid steel bars.

If only she could get them wide enough to slip out, then she could make a plan to gather all her winter gear while her mother sleeps and try her luck in the storm.

She looks at the touch lamp on the dresser and wonders if her efforts would be better spent smashing the glass panes or, better yet, arming herself against Sylvie. Maybe, just *maybe*, she could ambush Sylvie and knock the woman out. Then it would just be a matter of getting the car keys and her cellphone and escaping in the storm.

While she likes the last half of the plan, the first part gives her cause for concern. If she doesn't hit Sylvie exactly right, then—best case scenario—she risks killing her or—worst case scenario—she risks royally pissing her off with a lamp to the head. The last thing she wants is to get hurt worse than she already is. If her planned ambush ends in a direct one-on-one fight, Miller seriously doubts she'd win in the condition she's in.

Thankfully, she has another plan in mind.

Unfortunately, it only works if Sylvie lets her out of the room.

Deciding her only option is to wait, Miller lies on her uncomfortably small bed, elevating her foot as high as she can get it on her flat stack of pillows, and tries to nap.

SATURDAY, JANUARY 15, 7:14 P.M.

Miller stares at the ceiling of her bedroom, trying not to laugh at the absurdity of her situation. She knows it's not funny. She knows it's just the fear of what's happening to her and how powerless she feels trapped in her bedroom inside the cabin, but she can't help herself and a giggle escapes anyway.

She remembers staring at a ceiling similar to this one when she was growing up. She wasn't an especially difficult child, but her mother had made a point of punishing her for every inconvenience when her father was out of town. Miller has always wondered if her mother locked her away in her room to get back at her for her father loving his daughter more than he loved Sylvie. It's the same reason she suspects Sylvie had refused to hold down a job while her dad was sick: because he would have forgotten her first.

I wish it had been—

The lock outside her room clicks open.

Miller props herself up on her elbows, waiting for Sylvie to open the door. When it stays closed, she wonders at first if she misheard her mother on the other side or if her mother is baiting her into trying to escape. Deciding to play it safe, she lays back down on the bed and waits for Sylvie to open the door.

Luckily, she doesn't have to wait long. The handle turns slowly and Sylvie pushes the door open. She doesn't smile when she sees her daughter; instead, she crosses her arms over her chest and opens her mouth.

Miller doesn't give her a chance to talk. She knows if she does, her whole plan is ruined.

"I'm sorry, *Mom*," she says. Sylvie closes her mouth and stares at Miller in surprise. "I was rude. Like, *really* rude. You've been trying so hard and I've been really ungrateful about everything. And, yeah, I was mad about what happened with the snowshoes and everything, but it was an accident. I know you didn't mean to. You're my mom; you'd never try to hurt me. And I just… I've been really unfair and mean and just… *cruel*. I'm sorry."

Miller does her best to look sincere, going so far as to make eye contact with Sylvie before looking away, affecting shyness. She's grateful for the slow and steady stream of tears that have been leaking from her eyes all afternoon. She's not sure why her eyes won't stop watering—although it's a safe bet it has something to do with her broken nose and head trauma—but she's happy for the tears. They help sell the lie.

"Oh, sweetie," Sylvie says, crossing the room and getting on her knees next to the small bed. "That's all I wanted. I just… I miss us," she confesses.

"What do you mean?"

"It's just, it's been so long since you've been my little girl. Ever since you met that hussy," Miller knows she means Florence, "you've been different. You're argumentative, you don't listen, you've cut me out of your life."

"Yeah," Miller says sadly, nodding along with Sylvie's admission. Her mother either fails to understand or chooses not to: it's not that Miller is argumentative, she just stopped blindly agreeing with her mother; she hasn't been ignoring her mother, she's just trying to live her own life; she didn't cut her mother out, she just set boundaries.

"But now, *here*, we can be a family again. Just the three of us. Together forever."

The words don't sit well with Miller, but she smiles through the tears, praying her nerve doesn't fail her now.

"I'd really like that, Mom."

Sylvie leans forward and Miller exhales slowly, hugging her back as she fights her reflex to pull out of reach.

"Hungry for supper?" Sylvie asks.

"Yeah, starving."

"I made your favourite!" Sylvie says, helping Miller fully sit up.

"Oh?"

Sylvie nods as Miller swings her good leg out of the bed before gently placing her sore one firmly on the ground. She makes sure her feet are planted solidly, hoping things go to plan. Her mother wraps an arm around her waist and lifts her to her feet. She takes a step forward, but Miller stops her.

"Can I hold onto your shoulder from behind?" she asks, her heart hammering so hard against her chest that it shakes her back teeth. "I think it would be helpful if I practised putting my full weight on the leg, but I still need some support."

"Well just try not to lean too far to the left and you should be fine," Sylvie says, taking a small step forward, her arm still wrapped around Miller.

"I know myself, I'm absolutely going to lean too hard. Please, Mom?" she asks again, emphasising the word 'mom.'

Sylvie can't resist. "Sure, sweetie."

She lets go of Miller and gets in front of her, making sure she's close enough for her daughter to grab onto. She doesn't notice the empty pillow case on the bed, or how Miller awkwardly reaches for it before turning her attention to Sylvie's back. She just waits for Miller to hold on.

But she doesn't hold on.

Instead, she holds the pillowcase with both hands, the fabric pulled taut like a rope, and loops it under Sylvie's chin. She pulls hard, the fabric tightening around her mother's neck, cutting off her air. As expected, Sylvie panics and flails, trying to break out of the bind. She tries pulling herself forward, but that only works against her as she chokes worse. She then throws her weight backwards, but Miller is expecting this, and she lands back on her bed while Sylvie hangs awkwardly off the edge.

Knowing that this is her chance to give it everything, Miller leans back on her bed and digs her good leg into the floor, trying to make the pillowcase as tight as she can around her mother's neck. Sylvie gasps and gurgles, her tongue lolling out of her mouth as her flailing gets slower, weaker, and eventually stops altogether.

Miller holds the pillowcase tight for a moment longer, before giving it some slack. Sylvie is still breathing, she can see the rise and fall of her mother's chest, but she's unconscious. Once Miller's convinced her mother isn't about to get up, she reaches into the woman's pants pocket and looks for the car keys.

They're not there.

"No," she says to herself, frantically checking Sylvie's pockets for the car keys.

She finds the silver key to the house—the same one she suspects was used to lock her in her room—but the car keys are nowhere to be found.

"Fuck!" she screams, her loud voice echoing off the walls of the silent cabin.

She grabs the pillowcase with both hands and pulls again, holding tight for a few seconds before letting go. She doesn't want to kill Sylvie, but she doesn't know how long the woman will be out. Back when she was in school, a friend of hers used to have fainting spells, but she'd only be out for a couple of seconds. She's hopeful that her mother will stay out for longer, but doesn't want to take any unnecessary risks.

Miller pushes herself off of the bed and limps her way out of the room, bracing herself on anything that will support her weight as she moves. When she gets to the door, she closes it firmly and locks it with Sylvie's key before turning her attention to the task at hand: finding the car keys.

She stumbles through the hallway and into the living room. She can't help but pause in front of the photos on the wall, wondering what her father would think of all this. Would he understand that she has to get out, has to run, has to escape? Or would he tell her to give her mother a chance? Would he lie, like he always did when he'd try to make peace between them, and tell her that her mother just wanted what was best for her?

She pretends like she doesn't know the answer.

As she stumbles through the room, checking the coffee table and sofa for the car keys, she tries not to look up at the myriad of Sylvies and Millers who look down on her from their portraits.

She knows what they'd say to her.

Finding nothing in the living room, she makes her way to the front door—her mother's coat pockets and snow pants are empty—before finding herself in the kitchen. Her heart catches in her throat when she sees the supper that Sylvie's made for her: roast beef, baked potatoes, roast veggies, and Yorkshire pie… it's what she used to make when Miller and her dad would come home from ice fishing. She closes her eyes and breathes the fragrant dinner in and for the briefest of moments, Miller swears she's back home with her parents. Any minute now, she'll hear her father brag about the fish she caught, describing it as twice as big and twice as heavy as it really was while her mom acts impressed in all the right spots.

The pang of guilt that shoots through her nearly knocks Miller to her knees. She grabs one of the familiar chairs and sinks down, sobbing into her hands.

Part of her wants to limp back to the bedroom and unlock the door, climb into bed, and pretend like nothing's happened. Or, worse, act like she's to blame and grovel for her mother's forgiveness. Another part of her knows that the only way forward is out and that turning back is not an option. Her injured leg and bloody face remind her of that.

I wish it had been—

There's a slow and halfhearted banging from down the hall and Miller jumps in her seat.

Sylvie is awake.

"Sweetie?" her mother calls out, sounding confused as she slaps the door with an open hand. "Miller? What… Miller, what's going on?" she calls. Her voice sounds hoarse and quiet, and she stops calling her daughter just long enough to cough. "Miller?" she calls again, this time a little louder.

Miller doesn't have time to waste.

She pushes herself out of the chair and continues searching the kitchen for the car keys, her mother getting louder and louder from the end of the hall, fists banging harder against the door to the bedroom.

Deciding there's nothing for her downstairs, Miller turns her attention to her mother's room on the second storey. The stairs are hard to navigate and Miller clings to the railing for dear life. The last thing she wants is to fall and hurt her leg worse than it already is. With each step, her mother gets louder, more frantic, more vitriolic.

"Let me out!" Sylvie shrieks from the bedroom. "You bitch! You *bitch*!"

Miller takes a second to catch her breath at the top of the stairs, but that's all she gets as the banging from downstairs suddenly stops followed by the loud crash of glass breaking.

Confused, Miller listens for her mother's screams, but is met with silence. She stands still, straining her ears as she tries to hear her mother before she realises what's happened: Sylvie has broken out of the window and Miller has left the front door unlocked.

"Fuck," she yells to herself, rushing to her mother's room.

For a moment, she debates checking the empty room across the hall, but with increasingly limited time on her hands, she turns her attention to the locked door and jams the silver key in the lock. Although she can't smell the rancid air outside the bedroom thanks to her broken nose, she can taste it on her tongue. It's thick and bitter and tastes like sweat.

The front door swings open.

"What do you think you're doing?" her mother shouts to her, slamming the door closed behind her. "Get away from my room!"

Miller fidgets with the key, struggling to get the lock open. She looks over her shoulder and sees Sylvie at the base of the stairs snarling up at her. The woman is almost unrecognisable.

A massive bruise runs across her neck, turning the skin a garish mixture of deep reds and violet. Her eyes are tinted pink with scarlet spots peppering what should be the white parts of them. Her eyelids and cheeks are also stained red from the strangulation. Her hands are a mess, the skin on the knuckles and palms ripped and raw from beating the door bloody. There are cuts along her arms and legs, her jeans and long-sleeve shirt ripped from the jagged glass that she broke through and climbed over. Her shoulder rests at an awkward angle, likely from the eight-foot drop Sylvie took out of the bedroom window. Blood mixes with melted snow, forming pink puddles around her feet. She leans against the front door, lifting a foot. She winces as she pulls out a shard of glass embedded in her skin.

Miller frantically turns the key, trying to get the metal to un-stick in the lock and open for her.

"If you thought you were grounded before," Sylvie chuckles, "it's nothing, *nothing*, compared to how grounded you are now. I'm talking no television, curfew at eight, locked in your room for the next two weeks. Got it, missy?" She limps towards the staircase. With each step closer that Sylvie takes, Miller can hear glass scratch against the hardwood flooring.

"I said, get away from my room!" Sylvie shouts, footsteps getting faster.

Miller throws her weight into the door for all she's worth as the lock clicks, and the heavy wooden door swings open. She loses her balance and falls forward into the room, landing on her bad knee on the ground at the foot of the bed.

She screams.

At first, it's just from the pain that shoots through her body like an electric current. But then, it's from the sight that awaits her inside the room: the source of the putrid air.

Her father's body lies in the bed.

His skin is leathery and dry, but where it should be sunken in or hollow, it looks full and solid, like Sylvie has stuffed him with filling. His eyes are shrivelled and dry, black spots that watch her in the dim light of the room, and his mouth hangs open, the stitches that had been used to keep it closed during his funeral cut open and pulled out. He wears a pair of plaid pyjama pants, a white t-shirt, and his favourite beige loafers. His silver glasses rest on the brim of his nose, his leather watch strapped onto his too-bony wrist.

"Stop shouting," Sylvie snaps at her from the top of the stairs. "You're going to wake him up. For Christ's sake, he needs his rest!"

His head is propped up with a pillow and the blankets have been arranged around him like he's taking a nap. The bed next to him is worn in and messy from where Sylvie has been sleeping at night. On her bedside table rests Miller's phone and the keys to the Yaris.

"Stop being so selfish!" Sylvie pleads, voice hushed to not rouse her dead spouse. "He's been so exhausted lately. He needs to sleep. Just let him sleep!"

Miller grabs the edge of the bed and pulls herself up despite the pain coursing through her leg. She throws herself at the keys as Sylvie rushes into the room behind her, trying to grab her. Although Miller misses her phone, she manages to swipe the car keys off the small table as she falls to the floor.

"You can't go out in the storm!" Sylvie spits, running at her. "It's too dangerous! You need to stay here! You need to be where it's safe!"

Without thinking, Miller kicks her good leg out hard at her mother. Her foot connects with Sylvie's gut and the older woman crumples in two, wheezing. Miller kicks out at her again, and this time her foot crashes into Sylvie's temple, and the woman falls limp to the floor, out cold.

Miller drags herself past Sylvie and into the hallway. She can't help but take a final look back at her father. Sylvie said he was sleeping, resting peacefully in the bed.

From Miller's spot on the blood-streaked floor, it looks more like he's screaming.

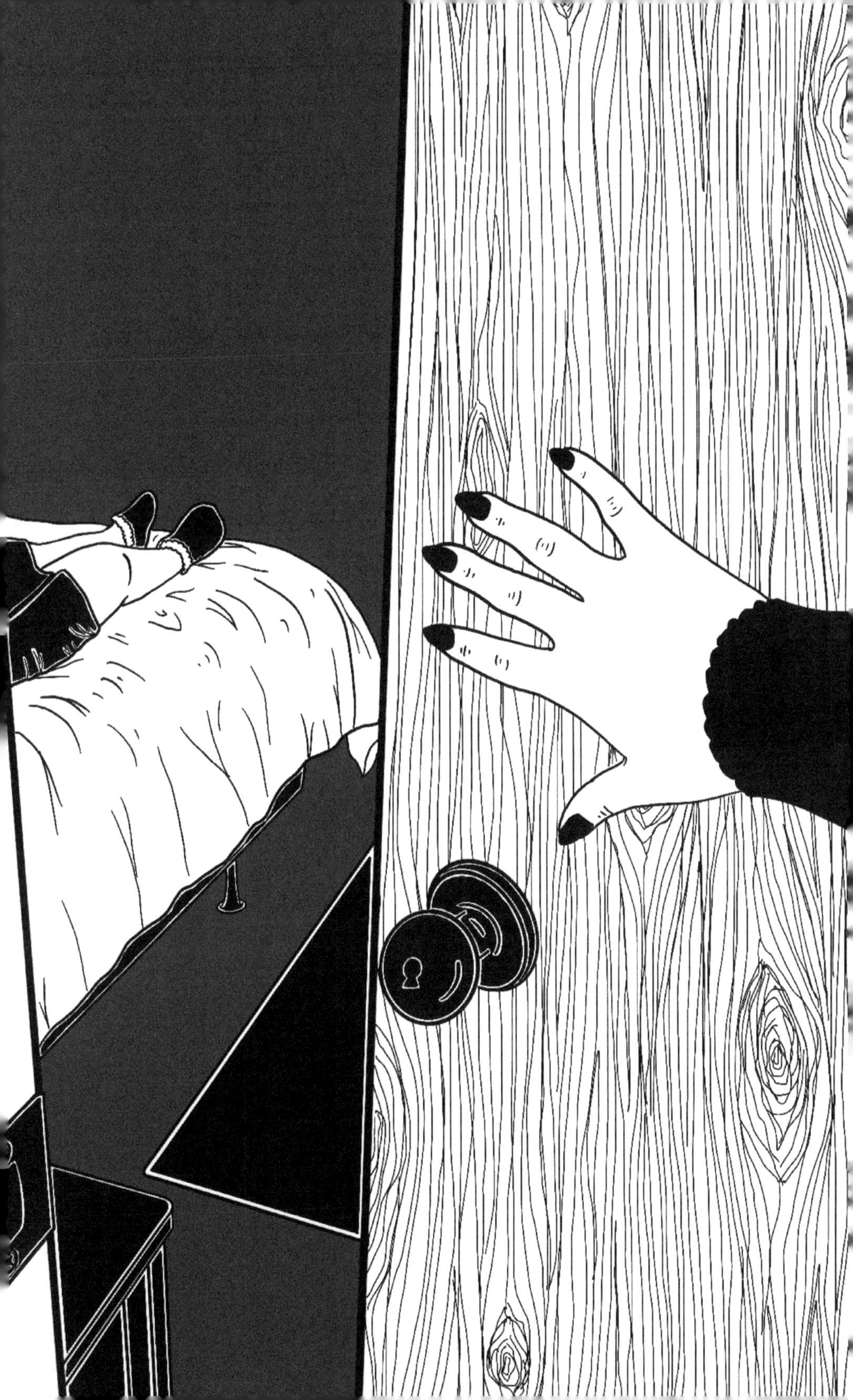

She manages to scoot down the stairs, moving as fast as she can without being reckless. The wind howls through the open front door, blowing the heavy snow into the cabin. Miller shivers as she gets to the base of the staircase, using the bannister to pull herself up and leaning against the walls as she stumbles to the entranceway.

She walks through the dusting of snow that coats the floor, her feet cold and soaking wet by the time she finally gets to her boots and shoves them on. She goes to throw on her coat—remembering it's still soiled with blood and forgotten in a black garbage bag—and throws on her mother's jacket instead.

She puts the car keys in the breast pocket of the coat and heads out into the storm.

SATURDAY, JANUARY 15, 8:02 P.M.

The process is painful and slow as Miller makes her way through the dense powder, one foot in front of the other as she carves a path to the car. With nothing to help support her, she's forced to put her full weight on her injured knee as she uses her good leg to break the snow ahead of her. Although her boots keep her feet mostly warm, her exposed legs and hands sting from the cold air, and both the back of her nightgown and legs are frozen from having to slide down the front steps of the cabin.

Her mother calls her name in the distance.

She moves faster.

Miller presses the button on the key again, a thin yellow light blinking through the darkness up ahead. She doesn't want to wear out the battery, but she also needs the light to guide her through the whiteout even if she knows it's helping to guide her mother too.

She moves forward and bumps into the car, thankful to have hit it with her good leg; she's not sure how much more pain she can take before she finally passes out from it. She rubs her right arm against the windshield, clearing some of the snow from the glass as she unlocks the vehicle. She knows that snow will be covering the glass again by the time she gets in, but she can't help herself. She climbs into the driver's seat and closes the door behind her, making sure to lock the doors before starting the car.

She puts the key in the ignition and turns it. The car struggles to start, but it eventually revs to life. It's the most beautiful sound she's ever heard. If she wasn't so tired, Miller would cry with relief. She holds the brake pedal down with one foot and grabs the gear shift, moving the car from 'park' to 'reverse.'

Sylvie slams her body against the hood of the car, her hands beating against the metal furiously.

“Get out of the car THIS INSTANT!” she wails through the windows. “You can’t leave now! It’s too dangerous! Your father is worried sick about you!”

Miller slams down the gas pedal, the tires spinning in place before the Yaris lurches backwards down the hill.

Her mother slides off the hood of the car, shouting after her. "You promised you'd try!"

Miller slams her foot on the brake, puts the car into 'drive,' and turns the vehicle around to point the nose of it down the mountain. She doesn't know where Sylvie is or if she's about to hit her.

She doesn't care.

Miller slams her foot back onto the gas and takes off down the hill, trying to remember the path back to the road.

“You can’t go! You can’t! Miller, YOU PROMISED!” her mother screams, voice far away and fading fast.

The snow falls in sheets and blocks out the sky, the world erased from view. As she swerves along the road, the side of the car scraping roughly against thick branches, she knows she should slow down.

But she can’t.

She’s scared if she stops for even a moment, Sylvie will find her.

She presses the gas pedal flat against the floor of the car as the small vehicle quickly gains momentum. It slides over ice and cuts through the snow, branches reaching for Miller and slamming into the windows. She grips the steering wheel, knuckles white, and she wrestles for control of the car as it moves forward with a mind of its own, crashing into a tree.

The last thing Miller sees as she flies through the windshield is white.

SATURDAY, JANUARY 15, 9:58 P.M.

Miller stares up at the sky, her breath swirling around her in silver tendrils. She tries to move her hands, her legs, *anything*, but her body is still.

Branches move over her head. She watches them slide in and out of view. On either side of her head she sees snow. Thick, cold, heavy, red snow.

She looks back up at the clouds overhead. For a moment, she swears she can see the stars through the white.

SUNDAY, JANUARY 16, 12:11 A.M.

The voice drones on and on, a constant hum in Miller's ears. She's not sure what the woman says. She doesn't really care.

Everything hurts too much for her to focus.

Someone leans her forward in the bathtub, patting her body dry with a towel before grabbing her under the arms and lifting her, dragging her body over the lip of the tub and onto the tiled floor of the bathroom. Miller sobs, bones aching from the movement. She can't see her own face, but she's willing to guess it's covered in thick gashes and scrapes like the rest of her is.

Sylvie pulls the sky blue nightgown over her head before pulling each of Miller's arms through the holes and wiggling it down over the rest of her naked body. Red spots bloom against the pale cotton, but her mother doesn't seem to mind. Sylvie runs a brush through Miller's hair, the bristles getting stuck on knots, pulling out strands of her curly hair. Once she's done, she fixes Miller's hair into braided pigtails and stares down at her admiringly.

"Look at you," she whispers. "My sweet baby girl."

Unable to move, Miller just looks up at her mother.

With a smile, Sylvie grabs Miller's arms and drags her out of the bathroom, and down the hall into the living room. The pictures watch her with black eyes and dead smiles as Sylvie pulls her up the stairs of the cabin to the second floor. It's a slow task, and each step causes Miller a fresh wave of pain.

"I think I'm going to put you on a diet," Sylvie says casually. "If you were even ten pounds lighter, this would be *so* much easier."

Miller just stares straight ahead.

"Don't worry, Mommy's here. I'm going to take care of you."

Her mother drags her into the master bedroom and then up onto the bed, arranging her next to the body of her father on top of the blankets. Sylvie then reaches across and tilts her husband's body so that he's angled towards Miller in the centre of the bed, his putrid skin pressed against hers. Sylvie gets onto the covers too, the three of them lying together the way they used to whenever Miller crept into their room after a bad dream.

"My sweet baby girl," Sylvie coos. "It's going to be okay. I'm going to take care of you and we'll get to be a family again. Just the three of us."

Miller stares at the ceiling, trapped between her parents as the storm rages on outside.

"It should have been you," she finally says, voice cracking. "I wish it had been you."

THE END?

WAIT, THERE'S MORE...

A NOTE FROM DARKLIT PRESS

All of us at DarkLit Press want to thank you for taking the time to read this book. Words cannot describe how grateful we are knowing that you spent your valuable time and hard-earned money on our publication. We appreciate any and all feedback from readers, good or bad. Reviews are extremely helpful for indie authors and small businesses (like us). We hope you'll take a moment to share your thoughts on Goodreads and/or BookBub.

You can also find us on all the major social platforms including Facebook, Instagram, and Twitter. Our horror community newsletter comes jam-packed with giveaways, free or deeply discounted books, deals on apparel, writing opportunities, and insights from genre enthusiasts.

ACKNOWLEDGEMENTS

If someone asked me (even just a year ago) if I thought I'd be writing the acknowledgements to my first novella, I'd have laughed myself hoarse. I'm incredibly thankful that past-Caitlin was horribly short-sighted.

Writing *This Is Where We Talk Things Out* was one of the most rewarding experiences of my life, and working with Andrew on this project has been a dream come true. I'm always blown away when someone has faith in my work, and it's because of people like him that I have the privilege to keep doing what I do. I really can't thank him and DarkLit Press enough.

I'd also be horribly remiss if I didn't thank my family, my friends, and my partner. I wouldn't be where I am today if not for their unconditional love, their unwavering support, and the truly staggering number of hours they put in listening to me read my work over and over again. I love you all so much more than you'll ever know.

And lastly, thank you to everyone in the writing and horror communities who've supported and believed in me over the years. I hope I can keep writing things that bring you joy, fear, and everything in between.

ABOUT THE AUTHOR

Caitlin Marceau is a queer author and lecturer based in Montreal. She holds a Bachelor of Arts in Creative Writing, is an Active Member of the Horror Writers Association, and has spoken about genre literature at several Canadian conventions. She spends most of her time writing horror and experimental fiction, but has also been published for poetry as well as creative non-fiction. Her work includes Palimpsest, 23 McCormick Road, Magnum Opus, and her debut novella, This Is Where We Talk Things Out. Her collection, Femina, is slated for publication later this year. For more, check out CaitlinMarceau.ca.

CONTENT WARNINGS

Mental Illness

Familial Trauma

Fatphobia

Violence

Death

DARKLIT
PRESS

Printed in the USA
CPSIA information can be obtained
at www.ICGtesting.com
LVHW012148120824
788094LV00027B/754

9 781738 658503